WHO IS MARTHA?

Marjana Gaponenko

Translated by Arabella Spencer

NEW VESSEL PRESS

NEW YORK

WHO IS MARTHA?

New Vessel Press

www.newvesselpress.com

First published in German in 2012 as *Wer ist Martha?*
Copyright © Suhrkamp Verlag
Translation Copyright © 2014 New Vessel Press

The translation of this work was supported by a grant from the Goethe-
Institut which is funded by the German Ministry of Foreign Affairs.

Library of Congress Cataloging-in-Publication Data
Gaponenko, Marjana
[Wer ist Martha? English]
Who is Martha/ Marjana Gaponenko; translation by Arabella Spencer.
p. cm.
ISBN 978-1-939931-13-9
Library of Congress Control Number 2014936217
I. Germany -- Fiction.

for Asti and Valbon

.... looking up, I observed a very slight and graceful hawk, like a nighthawk, alternately soaring like a ripple and tumbling a rod or two over and over ... It appeared to have no companion in the universe, — sporting there alone, — and to need none but the morning and the ether with which it played. It was not lonely, but made all the earth lonely beneath it.

Henry David Thoreau, *Walden*, 1854

The tyranny of reason, perhaps the most unshakeable of all tyrannies, still lies ahead of the world ... the more noble and exquisite the thing, the more devilish its misappropriation. Burning and flooding, the harmful effects of fire and water, are nothing compared to the havoc that reason will cause.

Georg Forster, to his wife in Neuchâtel, 1793

I

LOVE IS COLD. LOVE IS COLD. BUT IN THE GRAVE WE burn and melt to gold ... Levadski waited for the tears. The tears didn't come. In spite of this he wiped his face. Disgusting!

With a fixed stare he had just put the receiver on its cradle. What else, if not impatience, had he sensed in the breathing of his family doctor? Impatience and the buzzing of thoughts that had nothing to do with him, Levadski: Mustn't forget the baking powder ... moth repellent, furniture polish, what else? ... He could smell his own tiresomeness through the receiver. Breathe in, breathe out. Hang up, old man, hang up ...

Levadski went into the bathroom and threw up. He was overcome by tears. Whimpering, Levadski vomited for the first time in ages. The last time it had happened to him, he had still been wearing knickers. What had the girl's name been? Maria? Sophia? The young girl had allowed her hand to be kissed by a man with a moustache. In front of her a slice of cake. Jealousy had grabbed the schoolboy Levadski by the throat. He had stopped in front of the window of the café, taken a bow and spilled the contents of his stomach onto the pavement. Touching his chest, he'd slowly assumed an upright position again.

The girl had looked straight through him, her dilated eyes filled with a delight not intended for him or the man with the moustache, solely for the slice of chocolate cake.

What made me touch my chest back then? In the mirror, Levadski was clinging on to a glass of water. Had my heart dropped to the pavement when I was throwing up, had my arms and legs failed me, I would have noticed that something was missing!

Levadski rinsed out his mouth, took the showerhead and aimed it at the dentures he spit out into the bath while throwing up and which now reminded him of a boat capsized in the sick. The jet of water jerkily inched the outrageously expensive and highly impractical ball-retained dentures in the direction of the plughole. He leaned forward and skeptically picked them up – a dead creature, from which a final prank was to be expected.

No, he did not want to encounter this girl again. If she were still alive she would either be blind or demented or confined to a wheelchair. What was her name again? Maria? Aida? Tamara?

After Levadski's performance in front of the window, had she finished her cake? It didn't matter.

A tablet dropped into the glass of water. After a brief deliberation, it started to fizz and circle: a drunken bee. Carefully Levadski let the dentures fall in after. Plop … Since he had acquired artificial teeth he found this sound soothing; perhaps this was connected to the fact that it invariably accompanied the arrival of the Sandman. This must have been where its magical sweetness came from. Plop … and Levadski's eyes would already be falling closed. Plop … and he was already whirring into the sunset on the scintillating wings of a rose beetle. What is sweeter than your chocolate cake, girl? Only sleep. And what is sweeter than sleep? Only death.

On the short and laborious way to the living room,

Levadski was annoyed to see his green telephone glowing as if nothing had happened, as if he, Luka Levadski, Professor Emeritus of Zoology, hadn't just had a death sentence pronounced down the receiver. "We need to talk about your results – at the hospital, right away." Levadski had understood. There was nothing left to discuss. Talk about what? If the results were okay then you didn't call on a Sunday around lunchtime when elderly patients were possibly enjoying their deepest sleep. You also didn't call if the results were bad. If you had any manners, as a doctor, you knocked on the door personally in order to convey the news of someone's death. The blood was still pounding in his temples. Come in! he said to the doctor at the other end of the line. Or had he merely thought it? More and more often Levadski caught himself barely able to distinguish between thought, speech and silence, and it was becoming less and less important to him.

In two shuffling steps he reached the middle of the living room. Levadski's books sat stiffly on the branches and twigs of an impressive library. In the dusty sunlight they seemed to be awaiting a small show; the books held their breath, word-for-word. Not today, Levadski thought. A rainbow-colored drop glistened at the tip of his nose before exploding on the parquet floor. Another shuffle and Levadski was already sitting in his rocking chair by the window.

He closed his eyes and was certain: he looked imposing like this, genuine and alive, just as he had in front of the café window. The way he was sitting there with the beam of sunlight on his chest. Or perhaps the beam wasn't a beam, but a spear driving through an old dragon's body? He smiled. If someone had observed his face at this moment they might have believed that a water-thin slice of lemon had dissolved beneath the old man's tongue. But there was nobody who could have seen Levadski's face.

Since he had started aging, he had always been alone.

He started to age as a small boy. He aged when a robin redbreast hopped onto his shoulder while he was mowing the lawn. Like the red sky in the morning. Like a freshly baked soft rosy loaf of bread, it perched on Levadski with its thin legs. The robin redbreast decorated him more than any medal. It made him a human being. An old man! Levadski's watch started to tick, growing louder and louder with every movement of the bird.

He aged when from the window of the school building he observed a jay hiding its booty. The way it let two acorns, one after the other, roll out of its throat, buried them in the ground and marked the spot with colorful leaves. The jay. The blue on the hem of its robe and its jet black sapphire eyes, nodding its head mischievously: Levadski, Levadski, I know that you know! Levadski aged when he gnawed at almost cold chicken drumsticks at weddings or funerals. He aged when with a spoon he dealt a breakfast egg a shattering blow. He aged when in the spa town of Yalta a black-headed gull snatched a piece of cake from his hand. "You have robbed me of the pleasure!" Levadski shouted after it, stamping his foot, and yet immediately knowing: Nothing and nobody can take pleasure away from you. Pleasure is not a piece of cake. He aged especially on an autumn day when he stopped in front of an advertising column covered with film posters, threw back his head to read and was hit in the eye by pigeon droppings. Levadski was stabbed in the heart, in the middle of his aging heart. With every explosion of pigeon wings Levadski aged, with every daub of color that flew by, recognizable as a golden plover, blackbird or starling. He aged when he kissed a girl for the first time and suddenly in the dusk saw a shadow flit past. "I'll be damned! A pygmy owl!" he shouted into the frightened, astonished eyes of the girl, and he aged, turning a little more into the

Levadski he was later to become.

In the end it was music that dealt the ripening old man the crushing blows. It devoured him and spit him out, only to devour him again. The child Levadski, the old man Levadski, too naïve to curse the day on which he imagined he found music. It found him, and it drove into him like an almighty whooping cough, making him more and more hunched, so that he squinted up at it more dwarfed than a dwarf. This is how Levadski wandered through life. His hunch grew like his awe for music and birds. Yet neither the music nor the birds thought about condemning Levadski.

Done, damn it! Levadski feebly tapped his scrawny thigh. So, the suspicion that he had carcinoma of the lung was confirmed! The patient and pseudo-respectful whispering of his doctor at the other end of the line had said as much. The news hit Levadski harder than it would have if the diagnosis had been roared down the receiver.

He would have liked to say a prayer, something sublime, but everything venerable seemed either unspeakable or defiled by mortal fear and self-pity. Impure, simply impure. Ultimately everything in this world referred to man, to man alone. Even in the purportedly altruistic stirring of the soul yapped a little I! I! I!, and a tiny actor stood whistling in the wings of the most deceptively genuine feelings. Disgusting, thought Levadski, you can't even face a stroke of fate candidly. He thought this and knew that another Levadski, as if to confirm his thought, hovered the height of a hat above him, amusing himself at this sight: an old man with lung cancer sitting in a rocking chair, with a pretentious strip of sunlight on his pigeon chest and how strange, all the particles of dust, how they danced in the ray of light making it visible in the first place.

Levadski pursed his lips and, in his mind, spit on the carpet. What was he still supposed to think, when what he knew of human beings filled him with disgust? This scrap of knowledge ruined his pleasure in the unknown, in the mysteries of nature that were yet to be revealed. That he would no longer come to discover them made him livid. May youth divine the secrets of creation; the thought triggered a dull pain. It was not that he begrudged the others, those left behind, the revelation, no. Levadski just thought that mankind, if anything, had a simulated reverence for the simple and the great. It was the simple and the great that he felt sorry for, because it was pure curiosity that led man to pursue the wonders of nature; every solemn gesture was pure hypocrisy; every action, even if it was a self-experiment with a deadly outcome or involved years of sacrifice in the name of science, was nothing but egotistical defiance, nothing but pure self-assertion.

Levadski rose trembling from the rocking chair. Even now he had lied: regardless of mankind, it was not the simple or the great he felt sorry for, but that he would be denied coming one step closer to this mystery. He was envious and jealous and he begrudged the others, knowing at heart that all effort was in vain – the mystery of life would just grow further out of reach, for as long as this world still existed.

I have tramped around on this globe for long enough, Levadski thought. He opened the balcony door and sat back down in the rocking chair. The dusty curtain enveloped the figure of its guest for a moment, the street air. The street itself entered Levadski's library, filled it with the bothersome yet welcome signs of life, the honking of car horns, the shouting of children and the perpetual hurry of women's heels. He could also hear snatches of a conversation between ravens: "I love you," "I love you too," "Feed me!" "Antonida! Put your trousers on! Now!"

Who Is Martha?

a mother's voice ordered. Levadski raised an eyebrow; when he was Antonida's age, names like hers didn't exist, and girls still wore skirts.

"Oh dear," Levadski sighed. Why the intimation of his imminent demise hadn't allowed him to die on the spot, but had instead stirred up a lot of dust was an enigma. His chin dropped to his chest like an empty drawer onto a table; there is nothing to be had here, thieves, leave me alone. He opened his mouth. The ray of sunlight now rummaged in his mouth. Levadski stuck out his tongue and rolled it back in. Birds are better than we are, he thought, not least because they are able to open their beaks properly, unlike human beings, whose mouths only open by dropping their bottom jaw; birds simultaneously raise their upper beak slightly!

Slowly Levadski shut his mouth again. He remembered that many decades ago he had observed a common redstart through a pair of binoculars with a fat tick close to its eye. The bird didn't seem bothered by the tick. On a sun-drenched wall, it gently quivered with its orange-colored tail in front of its bride. At the time, Levadski could have sworn that the female was smiling at the male while it trembled in courtship. He had always suspected that birds smiled. Now, sitting in his rocking chair, he suddenly realized how this worked: The female bird smiled at her sweetheart just by looking at him. In spite of the ugly tick close to its eye. By being near him, she was smiling at him.

The thought that his body was at the mercy of a parasite, that his lung had been thrown to a sea creature as food, made Levadski peevishly swing back and forth a couple of times in his rocking chair. I am at the mercy not only of that bloodsucker but also of a cocktail of chemicals if I let myself in for chemotherapy, thought Levadski, and clenched his fists.

He noticed that following the telephone conversation he far too frequently used inappropriate language, words that he had always avoided in his life, "bloodsucker" or "damn it." That he had even been sick was outrageous and a certain sign of his decay. Who cares, Levadski thought, if I kick the bucket soon. His eyes widened. There you have it, kick the bucket, that's the kind of language I hear myself using! I should just die! Die and rot! Levadski gestured dismissively, rose from the rocking chair with a groan and shuffled to the shelf with the medical books.

Cyclophosphamide, sounds like a criminal offense ... checks the multiplication of rapidly dividing cells. Side effects: nausea, vomiting, hair loss. May damage the nerves and kidneys and lead to loss of hearing, as well as an irreparable loss of motor function; suppresses bone marrow, can cause anemia and blindness. Well, Bon appétit. Levadski would have liked to call the doctor and chirp down the line.

Tjue-tjue
Ku-Kue-Kue—Ke-tschik-Ke-tschik!
Iju-Iju-Iju-Iju!
Tjue-i-i!

If the doctor had asked him what this was supposed to be, Levadski would have stuck with the truth: A female pygmy owl attracting its mate, you idiot! And hung up. He felt like a real rascal. At the age of ninety-six Levadski was game for playing a prank. The dusty lace curtain stretched towards him, slowly as if submerged in water, behind it the spruce that lay in front of his house, with a little gold in its green beard and birds, birds, birds that hopped, as voices, as light and shadow plays, from branch to branch, from tree to tree, from cloud to cloud, from day to day, angels, always among people.

Who Is Martha?

Levadski suddenly had the feeling he needed a walking stick. He leaned against his bookshelf, amazed he had been able to live without a walking stick up until now, shook his head and put this oversight down to being a scatterbrain.

"Adieu," said Levadski to the medical dictionary in his hand before he shut it. He looked around his apartment, undecided as to what he should do. Instead of watering the flowers, making himself some porridge, or dusting, he took a walk around the four corners of his library to calm his nerves.

The only thing that really seems to belong to man is the genuine. And the only genuine thing about man, Levadski thought, breathing on his magnifying glass, is his pride! He was proud of the bookshelves that filled the walls. Though this trait belonged to the department of deadly sins, how could it be bad and depraved if it was purer, more sincere and unselfish, than the love that man imagined himself capable of? It was only pride that had no foundation and needed no admirers to sustain itself. Maybe it did poison the soul. But it also elevated the humble species of man a little, albeit to dubious spheres, from whence it became aware of the flicker of an immeasurably greater providence. The most beautiful thing was: A single surge of pride banished any breeding ground for loneliness. So why shouldn't man commit this sin?

"So what if I was never capable of love?" Levadski asked the back of a slim volume with the tight gold lettering *Manual for the Domestication of Extremely Reluctant Parrots*. "At least I was capable of being proud, I was proud of you, little book. Just as love allegedly pulls the rug out from under lovers' feet, my pride pulled the rug out from under my feet. I didn't soar high or for long, so I didn't land on my beak, but softly and in my element – in my library. I was never disappointed ..."

Levadski would have liked to cry, but he suspected that these tears would have been on account of the doctor's phone call rather than the solemnity of the moment, and so forbade himself to. My decorum will be the death of me, thought Levadski, for even the most natural thing suddenly seemed inappropriate to him. Honesty, he said to his books, is a slippery customer, it always slips away methinks when we believe we are surrounded by it. Levadski breathed on the magnifying glass again and polished it on his sleeve. Methinks! What a way to express myself! That he had a long time ago thought of winning over the opposite sex with this pathetic affected behavior, when his head had been filled with nothing but the mating dances and brooding habits of birds, was something he did not want to be reminded about. But he did think about it, he thought about it with a hint of bitterness. After a fulfilling academic life he knew: Women would have interested him more if they hadn't constantly insisted on emphasizing that they were different from men. If they had been like female birds, a touch grayer and quieter than the males, perhaps they would have awakened his interest at the right time. Levadski would gladly have procreated with such a creature. Only he didn't know to what purpose.

Levadski took a book from the shelf and blew the dust from it. *Dictionary of the Language of Ravens* by Dupont de Nemours, incomplete edition. A French ornithologist colleague had hidden the facsimile inside a cake, smuggled it through the Iron Curtain in time for Levadski's seventieth birthday. Levadski's delight in the facsimile had gotten the better of his reason to such an extent that he kissed the Frenchman on his moustache in front of the entire professoriate. Somebody raised his glass, he could remember that, and said, "A kiss without a moustache is like an egg without salt!" Everybody drank to international friendship and raven research, the words "May the day come when …" and "A clear conscience should not be a utopia" rang out. People clinked glasses and patted each other on the back. "From the primeval fish to the bird: a stone's throw!"; "From the lungfish to the human: the bat of an eye!" They hoped he would gain many years of pleasure from this unique and scientifically speaking totally uninteresting book. His anniversary was at the same time a farewell. He left the university and the students – everything that he had never really been attached to – with the thought that he would not live much longer. "*Adieu, mon ami!*" Levadski had tried to joke when he stood opposite the Frenchman at the airport. The Frenchman nodded hastily and withdrew from Levadski's brotherly kiss feigning a coughing fit. In the airplane the man with the moustache suffered a heart attack. For a time, Levadski was under the illusion that he had brought about the demise of his French colleague with his collegial kiss. If he'd explained to him that it was the custom in his country, like a weak handshake in Central Europe, perhaps the good man wouldn't have died.

"Such a beautiful book," said Levadski. He said it loud enough for the other books to hear. "This, children, is how the destiny of a man fulfills itself," Levadski continued ceremoniously. "A stranger arrives, makes a present to a stranger and gives up the ghost!" The books listened as if Levadski hadn't already told this story twenty times. "When, you won't believe it, on that very day, I was thinking that *I* would have to die soon! Such a beautiful gift …"

Levadski opened the book and smoothed out the pages, his knuckles cracking. He made a cracking noise with every motion, he always had since he was a child. Even when he sighed or sneezed. Once he had a bout of hiccups where every hiccup was accompanied by a cracking noise and he kept on cracking. A whole day passed by like this. Levadski turned the pages of the dictionary with a great sense of pleasure.

Kra, Kre, Kro, Kron, Kronoj
Gra, Gres, Gros, Grons, Gronones
Krae, Krea, Kraa, Krona, Krones
Krao, Kroa, Kroä, Kronoe, Kronas
Kraon, Kreo, Kroo, Krono, Kronos

It's a blessing I know French, thought Levadski, otherwise I would have had to learn it at the age of seventy to read this gem of a book. Simply and unassumingly the content of the language of ravens had been scraped together and distributed over twenty-seven pages, silent and powerful. Levadski remembered the bad mood he had fallen into every time he read the dictionary. Every time he stumbled over the word which suggested that man, in his search for enlightenment, had possibly overlooked the decisive junction – a word from the language of ravens. Which one was it? Levadski turned the pages and felt a surge of heat creeping up his hunched back.

Kra (quietly, deliberately, talking to himself) – I am
Kra (quietly, drawn out) – I am fine; or I am ready
Kra (short staccato) – Leave me
Kra (tenderly, coquettishly) – Hello; or Wake up; or
    Excuse the tomfoolery
Kra (questioningly, long) – Is somebody there?
Which word was it then?
Krao (loud and demanding) – Hungry
Kroa (chokingly) – Thank you, thank you so much,
    such a pleasure
Karr (resolutely) – Adieu!
Kro …

Who Is Martha?

Kronos! Kronos was the word! "Let us fly" in the language of ravens, *chronos* in Greek. Levadski shut the book. It was this junction that mankind had rushed past, past its own kinsfolk – past its brother animal. And along with it, consideration of the existence of a common primeval language had been buried! "Dear books," Levadski said to his library, "that contemporary animal psychology stubbornly refuses to credit the higher vertebrates with the power of abstraction and a center of speech is not only a scandal. It is a disaster! The existence of a common primeval language is perfectly obvious. Tell me, does the animal give the impression of being apathetic? On the contrary, the animal looks lively and inquisitive, not because it has just laid an egg, but because it possesses language. Language ..." raved Levadski, craning his neck. "Just like us the animal has named and internalized all the objects and impressions known to it. Otherwise the animal would long ago have died in isolation, darkness and silence, and even its heightened animalism would not have been able to compensate for its lack of speech. The animal has made sense of the world like we have, by naming this world!"

Moist-eyed, Levadski shuffled along the bookshelves and continued in a more hushed tone: "When humanity started to hone its mental and manual skills and continued to improve them, a thick civilizing fog spread over us, so that we either thought ourselves close to God or abandoned by God. But, my God, how pathetic! All we ever did was widen the gap between him and us. Between the animals and ourselves."

Levadski spoke to his books as if to his most gifted students. "A common primeval language appears to be physiologically and philologically undisputed. But from where is philology meant to take the means to prove that animals have a faculty for speech and explore their grammar?" The approving silence of the books spurred Levadski's eloquence on. "The day will come," he continued, "when the dictionaries of animal language will no longer cause their authors to be taunted and ridiculed, but bring them fame and honor. The authors will demurely lower their eyes." Slightly embarrassed, Levadski stared at the floor on which balls of dust were being driven back and forth by the draft. "Despondent because they arrived too late at the thought of recognizing in the animal an equal neighbor, a friend who can be confidently ascribed a language and an immortal soul once again, after such a long time ..."

The books maintained their silence. Let us hope it is not too late to create this bond of friendship, Levadski wanted to say, but he only thought it to himself in silence.

II

Levadski decided to put on his Sunday best, to tie his favorite bow tie with the ornate red-billed choughs on it, and to make his way into the center of town. What had to be done was clear: buy a walking stick, visit a decent pastry shop and eat cake until a stabbing pain hit him in the jaw, until he felt alive, and that his life was not such a bad one either.

While he was getting dressed he made a host of other decisions: He would touch the waitress, if she were pretty, as if by accident. If a waiter served him, he would trip him up. He would never again call his family doctor, and if he should get in touch with him, Levadski would hang up with a spine-chilling howl. To hell with radiation therapy and all those other highly poisonous drugs. Instead, he would treat himself to a piece of chocolate cake every day in honor of his mother, a widow who, between the wars, had been in the habit of ordering chocolate cake for Levadski in Vienna's finest hotel.

"Yes," Levadski said to the mirror, spit into his hand and smoothed down the only thin and fairly long strand of hair he still possessed in the direction of the nape of his neck. How had he been able to get through life without a walking stick?! No wonder he had a limp; this would never have happened if he'd had a walking stick. On the way to the bus stop Levadski stopped several times to blow his nose. He decided that right up until the day he died, he would not use checkered handkerchiefs any more, only white ones he would buy in the center of town together with the walking stick, a hat and new shirts made from one hundred percent cotton. Anything but shirts with mother-of-pearl buttons were out of the question, thought Levadski, dropping himself into a seat on the bus meant for pregnant women and disabled people. A heavily pregnant woman sat down beside him. "I have had enough, you understand!" he said to the expectant mother, immediately turning away again; the woman was incredibly ugly. The bus stopped. Levadski got off, but he wasn't where he wanted to be. Poppycock! He was annoyed. Now I have to struggle across Friendship Square and along the entire Cosmonauts Streeet. I should have stayed on the bus for another two stops. Oh well, fresh air and God's blessing … merrily we roll along.

Beneath a chestnut tree a blind man stood plucking his guitar. Levadski resolutely made a beeline for him, pointing a finger in the air. "Watch out for the chestnuts, you don't want to get … " The blind man lowered his guitar and snarled. Levadski had stepped on his hat.

"Shove off!" the blind man hissed in a Mediterranean accent, "or I'll give you hell!" Levadski shrugged his shoulders and left. After a few steps he stopped and put a hand to his chest: his dentures weren't there.

They can only be at home, Levadski thought, suddenly feeling dog-tired. He headed in the direction of a bench, where three women with headscarves were sitting. One of them was knitting, the second was feeding a hobbling pigeon, the third was reading. Levadski intimated a bow and, coughing, took a seat beside the woman who was reading. "Hurray," said Levadski, wiped the sweat from his brow and peered into the book the old woman next to him was reading. "All the more remarkable is the constant temperature of just below 95 degrees in the brood nest of the bees. We can observe that in cold weather conditions the worker bees gather close together on the brood comb, covering the brood cells with their bodies, like little feather beds, thereby ensuring the minimum amount of heat loss possible; when it is very hot we see them sitting on the comb, fanning their wings ..."

Levadski was moved. He would have liked to shake the hand of the old lady with the bee book, as if she were an accomplice. With the left side of his body Levadski sensed that the woman was smiling. He felt her smile like a small blazing glow. He closed his eyes. His old friend the robin redbreast with the tick close to its eye sprang to his mind.

"Are you smiling because I just said hurray?" he asked, opening his eyes.

"Yes," said the lady and burst into an ominous fit of coughing. "Excuse me," she choked, "a crumb." The pigeon with the leg injury took a couple of steps backwards and stared at the coughing woman with distrust.

"Friendship Square used to be a treasure of the town," Levadski said. "It was at its most beautiful in winter. We youngsters would come here with buckets of water, lay down a patch of ice in front of the Monument to the General and skate to our heart's content." The coughing woman closed her book and kept on clearing her throat. Levadski took the opportunity to squint over at the title of the book. *Intelligible Science: On the Life of Bees.* The lady knitting and the lady who had befriended the pigeon made a point of looking away. Levadski sighed. How many girls had he kissed under the supervision of the General. On the neck like a bloodsucker. Yes, Friendship Square had been something special once; every blind man would have been pleased to be warned by caring fellow citizens of the falling chestnuts. And now? Ingratitude wherever you looked!

"You know," he said to his bench companion, "I used to think that people who said 'Everything used to be different' were dreadful. Now such people are brothers and sisters to me!"

A couple, closely entwined, wandered past the bench, looking like an animal on four hind legs. The open shoe-laces of their shoes whipped to the left and right, throwing up dust. "You wouldn't have seen a thing like that in my day," Levadski said in a purposely loud voice. The couple stopped, kissed and moved on. "Disgusting!" Levadski grumbled and licked his lips. The missing dentures were giving him a hard time. Slowly his muscles were starting to ache from talking. He was not used to talking so much. Five or six words directed at himself were usually the daily norm. The General was enthroned on his mighty horse. A magpie relieved itself on the man's uncovered head, its wings and tail feathers iridescent. "Chacker chacker," the magpie called and cumbersomely flew onto the tip of a fir tree close by. "A pretty animal," said Levadski, then turned to his neighbor and saw that she was gone. The woman with the knitting and the pigeon-lady had turned into two smoking students.

Levadski got up and continued on his way. What I desperately need is a stick with a silver handle, he thought while crossing Friendship Square, a silver handle where the evening sun can play. My God, all the things I have missed in my life! His mood improved with every cobble-stone he left behind him. Now and again he stopped and wiped the sweat from his face. He leaned against traffic light poles while waiting for them to turn green. He avoided the underpass. He skirted around the gypsies and the newspaper vendors. Everybody else made way

Who Is Martha?

for him, Luka Levadski, Professor Emeritus of Zoology. Neither respectfully, nor filled with repulsion, but mechanically, like water separating from oil. Cosmonauts Street yawned at him with its two rows of sycamore trees that led to the heart of the city; to the shops with the indispensable items: the silver walking stick, the shirts, the snow-white handkerchiefs and a fashionable bowler hat. If I don't watch out I will turn into a dandy, Levadski thought, gleefully balling his wrinkled hands into fists in his trouser pockets. He felt a tear welling up inside of him, round and large like a diving bell. Covered in sweat, Levadski got into a taxi. "To the end of the street, please," he said to the raised eyebrows of the taxi driver in the rear mirror, and leaned back with a wheezing sigh.

In response to the buxom saleslady's question as to what size he was, Levadski shrugged his narrow shoulders and asked to be measured. "I commissioned this excellent suit I am wearing shortly after the war, in London, at the royal outfitters, for the forty-second International Ornithological Congress," Levadski said with outstretched arms. His breath stirred one of the saleslady's thin curls, who, lips drawn in, was taking his chest measurements. "Back then I was a little taller and didn't have a hunch, but I was just as unspectacular in breadth as I am now." The saleslady wet her right index finger and started turning the pages of a style catalogue. "I haven't grown a bosom, either," Levadski tried joking.

"What color would you like the suit to be?" the saleslady asked, without giving him the time of day. "Dark blue, brown, black, light gray, charcoal, pinstripe, dark buttons, gold buttons?"

"Dark blue with dark buttons, please."

"And the lining?"

"Burgundy of course."

The saleslady disappeared behind a door in her clattering heels, shortly afterwards reappearing with a dark blue suit and an older colleague. The lady explained to him that fashionable suits did not have a burgundy lining but were either dark gray or old rose. "Old rose would be stylish, dark gray would be more suited to business."

"Then I will take old rose," said Levadski, who in times gone by would have blushed in a situation like this, in times gone by, when he found people who were in the habit of saying "in times gone by" dreadful.

Levadski also bought a pair of suspenders, a beige scarf made of Irish pure new wool, a dark blue silk scarf with a rocking horse pattern, a silk bow tie with bright red bullfinches set against a black background, a silk tie with roseate terns and anchors, as well as ten white cambric handkerchiefs with an indecipherable monogram consisting of a multitude of curlicues. He had a hard time with the shirts. What they had in stock was checked or striped, with horrible plastic buttons. "Out of the question!" Levadski was incensed. "I have worn that cheap stuff for ninety-six years. Let me at least die in style!"

The desire to die in luxury he had never lived in spread like wildfire within him. It grew within him and swallowed up his fear of death. The sudden desire for luxury robbed Levadski of any sense of respect for the seriousness of his situation and reduced his lung nibbled by cancer to a mere trifle.

"My God!" Levadski moaned, "Is it so difficult to find shirts with mother-of-pearl buttons in a city of millions?"

The buxom saleslady grabbed the receiver. "I will call our branch office, meanwhile please take a seat." Out of protest, Levadski leaned against the sales counter with a pain-ridden face and stared out of the window. In the to-ing and fro-ing of people in the street he noticed a big white poodle in front of a sidewalk advertising column sniffing at a poster. *Moscow Circus, Parachute Jumping Kamikaze Dogs Landing On The Back Of A Lion! Come And See Our New Fall Show!* The dog lifted a hind leg, signed the poster and trotted off. Levadski deliberated on what the dog had meant to say by making the gesture. To hell with art? I can do that too? Down with posters – Save the rainforest?

"Our branch on Frantsusky Boulevard stocks shirts with mother-of-pearl buttons. With a double cuff but, unfortunately, only in white," said the saleslady, clasping the receiver with her diamond-bedecked hand. Levadski noted with satisfaction that the telephone was an antiquated model with a cord and dial, like the one he had at home.

"Marvelous. Double cuffs would be wonderful!"

To the pitying gaze of the two sales ladies, Levadski did a twirl in front of the mirror in the new dark blue suit. Without hesitation, he kept the suit on – the style was called Dandy. While the two ladies packed his outfit from the ornithological conference into a suit box like a corpse, dexterously and to the sound of rustling tissue paper, he envisaged how he would step out onto the street in a minute, where the wind, upon catching sight of him, woud leave everything else untouched – leaves, newspaper shreds and empty plastic bottles – the wind would rush towards him with an insane pleasure and before the eyes of the world, it would air Levadski's delicate pink secret, the jacket lining.

Levadski bought the shirts with mother-of-pearl buttons and double cuffs in the branch on Frantsusky Boulevard. He was allowed to fish a complimentary pair of cufflinks out of a big round bowl. In a hat shop a few streets up he spent an hour trying on headwear. A bowler hat made Levadski look like an emaciated Churchill; mortified, he put it back on the counter. A homburg with an upturned rim didn't suit him either. The design made Levadski look like a wrinkly youth who had gotten drunk after failing an exam. Finally he let himself be persuaded by a style called Dreamer, a home-grown version of the Borsalino.

"Imposing," said the hat seller with a click of his tongue, "very distinguished."

"Where can I get a walking stick with a silver handle?" After five hours on his legs he felt more dead than alive. "Or better yet, where is the nearest pastry shop?"

"Just around the corner, right in front of the Memorial to the Orange Revolution. There's only one place you'll find the silver walking stick, at 5 Victory Avenue."

Levadski dragged himself to the pastry shop and ordered a piece of chocolate cake. As he was not wearing his dentures he swallowed the alcohol-dipped cherry decorating his cake without chewing it. Am I not a moving sight? thought Levadski. A bee landed on a carnation that was leaning against the rim of a vase. Strange, thought Levadski, you can keep a dog, a cat, a goldfish, a parrot, a trained thrush or a blackbird, some people keep a snake or even a spider at home, but you can't keep a lone bee. The bee dies without its folk. Oh, it is going to die anyway! Levadski put the fork down on the saucer and leaned back. The bee flew from the carnation onto Levadski's cake. Impertinently it showed him its behind.

Levadski watched the animal and remembered how he had ignited a dry bush in the Carpathians when he was a student of ornithology between the wars in order to attract the bee-eater. He had hoped that a little posse of these birds would appear in order to snap up the insects escaping from the fire, which is precisely what happened. With a short sharp "whoop" the red-eyed birds made the air around Levadski whirr. It was his first successful experiment. With bated breath Levadski watched as one of the birds caught a bee and crushed it against a branch in order to squeeze out its poison.

"Check, please!" The large behind of the waitress who was placing empty coffee cups on a tray at the next table reminded Levadski of one of his resolutions from this morning. When the waitress brought him the check Levadski patted her hip with a shaky hand. "A bee," he apologized, paid and left.

A taxi stood in front of the Memorial to the Orange Revolution. Levadski got in. "Victory Avenue, please. Number five." The taxi driver spit his cigarette butt out the window and drove off. "You know," Levadski said, hugging the shopping bags and suit box to his ribs, "I don't understand what the Memorial to the Orange Revolution is about. There was such media hype when it was inaugurated last year. There is a pedestal, but where is the memorial?"

"Modern art," replied the taxi driver and switched on the radio, from which the last note sung by a male choir was fading away. The taxi driver must have been embarrassed at having to talk to a toothless old man, although he was well over sixty himself. Or, he understood something about modern art and found the idea of an invisible memorial extremely fascinating.

"The same old story, like everything in this world," Levadski said dismissively. "This kind of provocation occurs every ten years. Always the same. If they had planted a tree on the pedestal, as a symbol of hope, let's say, the memorial would make much more of a statement."

The taxi sped towards Victory Avenue. "Number five," Levadski shouted in to the rear mirror, "did I already say that?" The taxi driver turned his radio down a little.

"Did you say something?"

"Number five," Levadski repeated, and with a groan lifted his behind in order to get to his wallet.

In the cane shop Levadski was shown a collection of high-quality walking sticks made of different materials. Several models in 925 sterling silver and a few silver-plated ones were among them. He admired the timeless elegance of Derby canes, appraised several handles in the shape of elaborate animal heads, was amazed by folding sticks with soft rubber grips, and finally decided on a black polished drinking stick with an eagle-throat handle in sterling silver and a built-in glass tube for liquids of his choice. Levadski was thrilled. What cancer, damn it, the cancer can eat itself! When he stepped out of the shop and onto the street, instead of laughing his heart out, he traced a jaunty half-circle with his drinking stick.

During the night Levadski dreamed of two arguing male hawfinches. One of them called out sharply "tzee-tzee," the other one a tinkling "tzaa-tzaa." Both of them stood in front of a pile of half-ripe peas in Levadski's mother's vegetable garden. "Shove off!" Levadski shouted out the window of his nursery and threatened the birds with a watering can. The birds carried on arguing with each other, feathers flew through the air, but the pile of peas remained untouched. "Shove off, you scoundrels!" Levadski shouted. The birds did not listen to him. He let his watering can drop and fluttered out the window. The birds froze and in amazement tore open their powerful beaks. As he couldn't think of anything better to do, he started juggling the peas. The birds forgot their quarrel and clapped their wings. Levadski was pleased and juggled faster and faster, clockwise. Then the two male hawfinches fluttered up and pecked at the peas with their beaks until there was nothing left to peck.

In the morning, still half asleep, Levadski remembered the telephone conversation with his family doctor and became sad. So it had not been a dream after all, he would die soon. But he had always known this, it was nothing new. If his mother were alive, he would have called her and asked whether he should submit himself to chemotherapy or not. His mother had always sworn by herbs, good deeds and thoughts, she wouldn't have batted an eyelid at the diagnosis and would just have baked delicious pastries until her death, Levadski thought, sitting up in bed. But perhaps she would have advised me, her only child, to do something different, considering the advancements in medicine? Oh, to hell with the cancer!

The stranger from the day before, the old lady with the book on bees, sprang to mind. That he was still capable of marveling at people was a good sign, a sign that he was not lost to himself or to the community. Thank goodness! Levadski thought, if I had not noticed the book, or if the lines on bees had no longer moved me – that would have been bad! Dear God, I thank you. Levadski folded his hands. For a number of years now he had been saying his morning prayer out loud, partly to reassure himself that he was still here and partly to exercise his vocal chords.

I have woken,
the sun has risen laughing,
peaceful was the night.
God our father,
you protected me.
Only you know
what the day may bring;
yet whatever that may be:
You will be with me.

Levadski wiped away a tear and in a faltering voice addressed the mark left by a bloodthirsty mosquito on the ceiling:

I will write it into my heart and mind,

That I am not alone unto myself on earth,
That I will pass on the love that sustains me
to others.

After breakfast he called his bank. His savings turned out not to be exorbitant, but quite substantial. My god, have I lived frugally! Levadski was pleased. He thought of his account in Vienna, to which royalties owed him for his articles in the Konrad Lorenz annual magazine had regularly been transferred since 1975. He had never withdrawn any, how could he have? The last time Levadski had been in Vienna was in 2002, at the Conference for the Advancement of the Mobility of the Northern Bald Ibis. He had not gotten around to withdrawing any money, he was much too busy, too much in demand. The Konrad Lorenz Institute welcomed him with open arms. He was a guest of state and had been invited by the Republic of Austria, had traveled first class, was served a hot meal on the plane and was collected by a black limousine. The chauffeur wore white gloves, like a waiter. The suite in the Hotel Imperial, where he had been put up like a king at the expense of the institute, had five crystal chandeliers. Levadski's neck ached from admiring the pomp. He liked to recollect this journey and the night at the Imperial. The northern bald ibis to whom he owed all this had already been wiped out across most of central Europe in the seventeenth century. The Konrad Lorenz Research Center set itself the task of making the ugly bird a native in its old home again. It worked, but the northern bald ibis no longer knew that it was meant to set off to Italy in the winter. At the conference Levadski suggested driving all the young birds south in the winter and when they grew older, flying ahead of them in light planes as a means of instruction, so that later they would be able to find the way themselves. The idea landed on fertile ground. Soon afterwards a flock of northern bald ibises set off for their Italian wintering grounds and returned safely in spring. Levadski was sent numerous newspaper articles: *Paving the way ahead, Ukrainian ornithologist breaks all barriers – Professor Levadski from Ukraine (born 1914) gives the northern bald ibis wings – Off to Italy! An enterprising idea changes the world of an exotic animal believed extinct – Foster father in a light plane: A Ukrainian sends the northern bald ibis on holiday – Away with the borders! Reintroduction into the wild project unparalleled in the history of wildlife conservation.*

Levadski put the kettle on the stove to make tea. He sat himself down on a kitchen stool. He stared at the gas flame. I will let the cancer be cancer, he thought, I am not wasting a single kopek on it. Instead, I will fly to Vienna. I will fly to my wintering grounds like a northern bald ibis. Into the eternal sun. One way with a tailwind.

The water boiled and hissing spilled over the rays of the blue gas sun. Levadski got up and turned off the gas. "Decided," he said and poured the water into his only unchipped china cup.

III

LEVADSKI WAS BORN THE ONLY CHILD OF A FATHER WHO was a forester in a count's woodland and a mother who was a Viennese ornithologist in East Galicia. The year of his birth was not a promising one for the world. In an American zoo, on the day of his birth, the last passenger pigeon died, a beautiful bird with red eyes and a black beak. That of all possible days, it was precisely on the 1st of September, 1914 that the bird drew its last breath, on the very same day that Levadski, smeared in blood and blind, mewing softly, announced his arrival, was something he learned only as an accomplished man, shortly after being conferred a doctorate. From that day forth he thought of Martha the passenger pigeon once a year, and of how lonely she must have been in captivity. Of course she had known she was the last of her kind. You just knew something like that. Irrespective of whether you were a human being or an animal. Things like that were whispered to you on thin air, straight into the heart. It was sheer mockery – of all birds, the passenger pigeon, a particularly social species, had to disappear from the face of the earth like this.

When Levadski's mouth was almost full of milk teeth, his father, who had lost his job, shot a bullet through his head beneath a spruce tree. The old count sent the widow a telegram from Vienna via the war post. DEAR MADAM STOP MY THOUGHTS ARE WITH YOU STOP A SHAME ABOUT YOUR HUSBAND STOP BE BRAVE STOP

When Levadski was able to sketch a bird on four legs, the Tsar abdicated in Russia, his personal cook poisoned himself, the Provisional Government was formed, Lenin, watched by ten thousand pairs of drunken farmers' eyes, dispatched big words into the frosty air, the landed gentry were dispossessed and churches were ransacked for the good of the people.

When Levadski's last milk tooth surfaced, the Bolsheviks brought down the Provisional Government. Little Russia declared its independence from Big Russia. "Why did you bring only me into the world?" Levadski asked his mother, who said to him: "So that you could become something special, my little one!"

But in reality it was the untimely disappearance of his father from the forest stage that allowed Levadski to become something special. "He loved the forest, till the very last!" Levadski's mother enthused. "The forest was his office he stepped in and out of at will, strode through for hours on end, in which he was permitted to shoot and spit on the ground. He would have withered away in the city," she said time after time, tearfully wiping her nose.

Of all the animals, Levadski's father loved birds the most. After his death, his young widow inherited a barely overseeable quantity of folders containing bird sketches. The deceased had drawn mallards, waterfowl and little grebes, wagtails, green woodpeckers and collared doves, buzzards, falcons, sparrowhawks, hawks and kites, tree pipits, meadow pipits and tawny pipits, as well as mistle thrushes, redwings, song thrushes and fieldfare. He hadn't shunned the great white heron, the night heron or the small white heron, either.

Before he sketched them, Levadski's father would fire a fine-grained shot at his models. He used minute pellets so as to cause as little damage as possible to the bodies. Then, with the use of wire, he would arrange the carcasses in a natural or dramatic pose and sketch them. *A stork devours a frog at sunset* was for the common people. *A stork with hair combed in a revolutionary manner across its brow gazes into the sky and is struck by lightning on the beak* – that one was intended solely for Levadski's father, for his own aesthetic pleasure. It was for this reason that Levadski's mother called her husband a Neoromantic. "In rejecting the natural, he braved it," she sighed. "He even spit in the face of the drawing tradition of the 18th century. Your father," she said to Levadski, wiping a tear from her widow's eye, "looked far back to the origins of animal worship, hoping for its rebirth. Look!" His mother solemnly grabbed one of the folders and pulled out a sketch.

"A stork," Levadski instantly remarked.

"A stork for you, a stork for me, a stork as such. But to your father," she wagged her finger, "it was a stork not struck by lightning, but kissed by it, yes, kissed by it. Suffused with light, the felicitous bird soars above the world in order to clack a delightful song – a representative of the genus of striding birds and at the same time, an angel. Both were not out of the question for your father, may he rest in peace ..."

My father was not a bad man, thought Levadski. The sharper his ornithological insight grew, the more this belief took root in him. When he started recognizing the birds that his father had painted out in the wild, he would have spit in anybody's face who said a bad word about the dead man. Levadski examined the bird sketches conscious of his father's gaze hiding behind every bird's eye, the face

Who Is Martha?

of a vibrant man, which without a doubt he must have been. "A person who observes birds knows the joy of living," Levadski's mother swore, scrunching up her slightly yellowed delicate handkerchief in her withered hand.

"My father was happy, he knew the joy of living!" Levadski shouted to the children in the village, when he believed he was met with a pitying look. Their fathers were farmers, blacksmiths, bakers and butchers, some, in the worst cases, had died in war, were crippled or missing. These children were to be pitied, not him, for his father had known the joy of living. In the evenings their mothers sent them to the tavern to fetch their fathers home from drinking. Levadski would linger close by, leaning against a wall. He was more proud than sad that his father was unable to stagger out of the tavern. He knew the joy of living, he shouted in his head at the children clutching their fathers' arms, Oh yes, he knew it.

"One day you too will know the birds," Levadski's mother promised. And one day this really was the case. Levadski knew them all, and he knew: the joy of living had nothing to do with the bullet his father had fired into his brain. This joy of living conjures up a space for a candid, totally unimpeded joy, smack in the middle of human destiny. This space floats within us like a bubble, and pleasure, its contents, absolves us from everything – our sins, our mistakes, it even pardons the most wretched end. One day Levadski was familiar with the birds and understood: once you have given yourself to the inhabitants of the sky, you are doomed to happiness. You can then happily fire a bullet into your brain.

In August, shortly before the fateful Battle of Amiens, Levadski could brush his teeth with tooth powder all by himself. The young widow decided to lock up the forest warden's house and to return to Vienna aboard a hospital train. Levadski watched as she took her axe and lopped the heads off all the hens and the old cock. The only reason why the birds had not landed in the stomachs of the marauding fighters in the interest of the right cause was because they had been kept in deep bunker-like cellars during the war years and not in the stable. Only at night, if you held an ear to the cold kitchen floor, could you hear them softly lamenting in their sleep. Singing, Levadski's mother loaded the carcasses of the birds onto the wheelbarrow and wheeled them, to a melancholy warbling tune, into the village to exchange them for gold with the neighbors. "Eat and remember us," Levadski's mother said at every threshold. Levadski wanted to say "Eat and remember us" in front of the last door, but nobody opened. So Levadski said it in front of the closed door.

"Died of starvation," explained Levadski's mother, who knew to interpret the sweet smell of decay as the old Jew's last greeting, "the poor little grandfather." They headed back. The last hen reproachfully puffed up the sack in the widow's hand. The old man was dead. Levadski wanted to know why.

"Did he not have anyone to cook for him?"

"He was a widower, just like I am a widow."

"What does that mean?"

"The male version of me. Do you understand that?"

"Yes."

"So if I am a widow, he is a widower, you see, an extended version of widow."

"Why couldn't the widower eat at the neighbors'?"

"Because he knew they didn't like him."

"Why?"

"Because he was not only a widower, but also an old Jew."

"What is an old Jew?"

"An old Jew is a colorful bird. Remember the bird

feeder we made out of fence posts last winter," Levadski's mother said, "and the two types of birds that always came to peck the kernels from the stand? The birds are called chickadees and nuthatches. Remember the way it was: the chickadee that was always there didn't want the other chickadee to eat any of the food and he pounced on his fellow bird. The chickadee left the nuthatches to eat in peace. It's the opposite with humans. They want to eat together. Birds of a different species are a thorn in their eye."

"But they are all birds!" shouted the little Levadski.

"Humans, you mean," his mother corrected him. "Oh, I don't understand anything anymore myself!"

When Levadski reached the forester's house with his mother, a veil had descended over the conversation. When he bent over the steaming chicken broth, the conversation about birds and humans sank like a chestnut in a mirrored lake. And when he sat in a train for the first time, between whimpering soldiers with bandaged arms, legs and heads, the picture of the widower behind the closed door was no longer even a circle of water in the pond of his memory.

Behind his mother's aunts was the stale air of their apartment, a silent third presence. Levadski greeted all three of them on the threshold with a bow and stumbled in. "This is where we are going to live," Levadski's mother announced, her eyes moist.

Several times a week Levadski ate cake with his great-aunts in the most beautiful hotel in Vienna. He ate cake until he had grown eight inches, he ate it for three whole years. After cake, Levadski devoured the golden sound of music. In the Golden Hall of the *Musikverein*, a few steps from the hotel, he was steeped in a pleasure even sweeter than chocolate cake.

IV

WHILE LEVADSKI'S MOTHER CHANGED THE DIAPERS OF elegant ladies' children and took them out for walks in their strollers in the fresh air, Levadski's great-aunts dragged the unexpected consolation of their old days into the *Musikverein*. On a thinly upholstered chair with his short legs dangling, he listened on long evenings to symphonic works, to concerts for piano and orchestra, for solo piano, for piano duets and for two pianos. He listened to secular and religious choral pieces with and without orchestra, and learned to appreciate the benefits of the cheapest balcony seats directly above the orchestra. The paneled ceiling formed a kind of resonant expanse that seemed to intensify the music, to gather it and hurl it down on nobody but Levadski.

"We are sitting in the belly of an architectural masterpiece," the great-aunts whispered to Levadski with sour breath. Solemn, for the golden notes of the hall were solemn, the blue ceiling fresco with Apollo's nine muses, the cool white of the sculptures above the balcony doors. Solemn were the movements of the violinists when they dabbed their beads of perspiration, solemn were the embroidered initials on their chin cloths. Incredibly solemn were the tear-stained faces of the music lovers that

Levadski could see from his cheap seat, shimmering in the discreet light of the crystal chandeliers: all the red noses that acquired a prophet-like dignity in these solemn surroundings.

"You will understand it one day," the sour breath of the great-aunts assured him. Levadski already understood now that music had to be a question of magic – what other possible explanation could there be for the two sisters seeming less ugly when the music began to play? Even during the intermissions it was an ugliness sugared in a soft golden dust that they radiated. The music itself was perfume! It smelled of the powder of his aunts' décolletées leaning over the balustrade, like polished brass plate and the sweat of the musicians.

While a rattling Rachmaninoff swept across the stage and the blurry-eyed music buffs wiped their noses, Levadski leaped through sun-drenched meadows of flowers, embraced thousand-year-old trees, nimbly flitted up their resinous trunks and drowned in oceans filled with fish. He couldn't know that one day music would be reduced to a three-tiered smell in his head. To the smell of powder, brass and sweat.

There sat Levadski, leaning against a cool pillar. When the music excited him too much, he would gently knock his head against the pillar. Most of the time a lady with binoculars sat next to him, taking up two seats. Through her binoculars she looked down on the oily bald heads of the double bass players and smiled mysteriously or licked her painted red lips. During the intermission she made up for her two cheap seats with a caviar canapé. When she directed her binoculars at the double bass players again after the intermission, a dark caviar egg hung in her smile. Right next to her sat an old man napping behind the pearly sheen of a pair of pince-nez. During brass-filled sections he would start up and finger his tailcoat – he was here. He was. He was he. And again sweet slumber beckoned – the old man succumbed to reveries until the next brass attack. Opposite Levadski on the other side of the concert hall a young emaciated girl sat swaying, opera glasses in hand. To the right and left of her, women with gray chignons were dozing. Beneath her were surging waves of the educated middle class with starched collars of a white immune to any kind of criticism in the subdued light.

"They used to crack open bottles of champagne here," one of the great-aunts sighed, "I miss the popping." Her breath drove into Levadski's left nostril in the form of a sour pickle.

"Much better," her sister whispered, "this way you can enjoy the intensity of the music more." And a second sour pickle blocked Levadski's right nostril. How blissfully he sneezed in the *Musikverein*! How blissful the pain of the repressed sneezing and the subsequent goose bumps!

It was in the *Musikverein* that Levadski for the first time also heard the conflicting descriptions that the music lovers gave to the music. Mouths concealed behind hands, leaning towards each other or sitting upright with glassy mad eyes directed at the orchestra, they declared of the music:

"Heavenly tootling!"

"Excruciating whining."

"Shush …"

"A spicy butchery of melodies."

"Vile harmonics, but interesting."

"Incredibly inflated. Still, nice instrumental effects."

"Deathly boring – the same rhythm over and over again."

"Be quiet!"

"A charming mess!"

Invisible occurrences were also noted.

"The double basses are dragging themselves laboriously."

"The violins are skulking."

"The blaring trumpets doubling up on the violins."

The music itself was inspired to action.

"But now, hop, hop, hop!"

"Stab and pull! Stab and pull!"

"Heeey, heeey get on with it!"

And many ambiguous notions were uttered in a state of euphoria.

"One wall of thunder after the other, how refreshing!"

"The indulgences of this genius transcend the spheres."

"Sugared water on my head, Lotte, I am flying!"

It was obvious: only a lover was capable of speaking about music like this, someone who really knew it. Levadski was surrounded by pure music lovers. Withered ladies with glittering dangling earrings belonged to this circle of lovers, youngsters with red cheeks and long aching fingers belonged, too. Sobbing chambermaids in plain dresses were friends of music, and even the clergy rolled their eyes up at the hollow paneled ceiling, grateful for music on earth and the gift of hearing.

The progenitors of music appeared to be the musicians on the stage. Damned to eternal reproduction, they were in the child Levadski's eyes nothing but soulless puppets.

It was not difficult to guess what the conductor's role was: the gate through which the sacred composer protruded his dragon's tongue. For the duration of a symphony, a concerto or a piano concert, the conductor appeared to relinquish his body and his personality. The conductor's pitted shell allowed something better than itself to rule and triumph. But on closer observation this turned out not to be the case. The conductor did after all inhabit his body. The reason for his writhing like a person possessed was frighteningly mundane: because he was torn back and forth between having to control himself and at the same time having to forget himself. The conductor was meant to follow the composer's blueprint but also his own ideas, his volatile temperament and the moment. Whom to do justice to? The composer, the audience, or himself? How could you not go mad in the process?

"The director of an orchestra," one of the great-aunts informed Levadski, "is a bureaucrat responsible for the correct measure, nothing more."

"An intelligent windmill rooted to the spot who'll never fly," her sister added.

Filled with sympathy, Levadski looked at the conductor, a mortal being, permanently in danger of slipping on the conductor's podium and toppling off in the heat of battle and besmirching the immortal music on account of his mortification. The pianist, the conductor's fellow sufferer, fared better in that respect: being seated, she was unable to stumble.

Where was the composer, Levadski wanted to know from his great-aunts. "Everywhere, my child, everywhere!" Levadski looked and marveled. Most of the time the composer, a curly-haired seraph, sat on God's shoulder, smiling bashfully at his much celebrated failings.

"It's getting exciting down there," the sisters said, speaking through their noses, their blurry gaze directed at the front rows in the hall. From the lofty perch of their cheap seats in the organ balcony they were in a good position to speak, for they knew its advantages: the view and the movement – everything that you couldn't deny yourself as a true music lover.

"Down there they don't get to experience the movement at all," they whispered in Levadski's ear. "... Not real music lovers ... A load of philistines. They don't even dare to cough, sitting there rusting in their patent leather shoes, all in the first rows for the sake of being seen, stiff and empty as they are … Pitiful!"

"In the old days," the sisters enthused, "champagne corks flew through the air, people joked and laughed to their heart's content, you paid the neighboring box a visit, a little tête-à-tête, a kiss on the hand, oh, and now? Now, without the bubbly, we have stepped slightly closer to the music …," remembering they were speaking in front of the innocent child Levadski. "Only the vanities remain the same old ones," they added.

From up high, Levadski marveled at all these people who monopolized his great-aunts' music. They must, Levadski suspected, have arrived at the enjoyment of music through a stroke of fate and forced the real music lovers into the cheap, if marvelous, seats in the balconies overlooking the stage by the organ. The pain of an unendurable loss could be seen in the hangdog expression on the two sisters' faces, precisely where the hangers-on sported a smile. This pain was of such magnitude that even the rays of music, the reason everyone was gathered here in the Golden Hall of the *Musikverein*, could not properly warm Levadski's great-aunts. Not least because they appeared to be continuing a silent battle from their organ balcony – the right of the firstborn had to be put on display for all to see, as an unmistakable pedagogic greeting to everyone down there. The aunts were only able to relax during the intermissions, in the circle of the old elite.

"At last among the like-minded!" the sisters sighed on the way to the buffet, wiping the dust from the marble steps with the hems of their shabby dresses. With a dignified impatience, holding Levadski by the hand, they hurried towards the people who understood music. They recognized each other from a distance, intimated a bow or a kiss on the hand; ladies wearing arm-length gloves shook each other's hands. You could see the sparkle of pocket watches on gold chains, wilting carnations in the buttonholes of gentlemen gave off a barely perceptible scent, so heavy were the clouds of perfume of the supposedly weaker sex who had done their best to dress up to the nines. People conversed during the intermissions as if this were the last opportunity to impart something of essence to the world. The topic of conversation was music; after all it brought the old elite together, veterans of an out-and-out lost and futile war. A folding fan dropped to the parquet floor, was picked up with a smile and a slight creaking of the spine, people continued to converse about music. People offered toasts to the music.

This group of people was even more suspect to Levadski than their opponents who, with champagne glasses filled to the brim, skirted around the island of the elites, as if they were ashamed of the course that history had taken. Levadski found it difficult to distinguish between the true and the false music lovers, for both clans were equally convinced of their love of the art. The hangers-on gave the impression of being clueless and inquisitive, which made them a little more sympathetic in Levadski's eyes than those who were of his great-aunts' ilk, so immersed in their knowledge of the essence that there seemed to be no room for music itself in their emotional life. In spite of this, Levadski's passion for music was kindled by these partially unintelligible conversations in the buffet hall of the *Musikverein*, in between the canapés with carefully counted caviar roe and the tinkling drops of crystal chandeliers warmed by the breath of the people, slowly circling around themselves. The *Musikverein* hall was gold, the pearls of the champagne were a dusty gold in the flutes, like wax candles forming a circle around the speaker with the gold tooth in his mouth. Levadski listened to him, hanging on every word. Like crumbs of gold, the man scattered his words into the circle of altar boys and girls holding wax candles in their hands.

"How, ladies and gentlemen, can music free itself from its fetters? From which fetters?, the eyes of the youngster (Levadski ducks) ask rightly. My friend! From which fetters? The answer is simple – from the fetters of its existence as a masterpiece! Called back into life through the palpable feelings of the interpreter. But, my dear sir, the charming ladies (looking over at Levadski's great-aunts) will object, what about fidelity to the work and the historically correct way of playing it? (Pauses for a drink, scans the circle with a mischievous glance.) Are we academic classicists? Do we belong to that pedantic breed of people who blindly believe that the work will speak for itself if the interpreter restrains his feelings and snatches those of the composer out of thin air? (Levadski's great-aunts shake their heads decisively.) No, no and no again! What an absurd thought! How, if not by means of a tender heart, is the musician meant to understand the composer? It is only through the living, through our presence, that the idea of a work can be realized. But (the prophet raises a chubby forefinger) how to play, in particular the younger ones among us ask (looking at the shrinking Levadski), in order to do the composer justice? Let us forget, dear friends, (conciliatory nodding of the head) our misgivings about the personal touch. A respectful virtuoso will never vainly abuse it. Where would that get us, yes, where would that get us? (Pauses for a drink, absent-minded wiping of the moustache.) The composer is dead! (Fixed stare into the circle.) Yet for as long as he lived, he found consolation in this one thought: his music will outlive him and be played by generations to follow. Irrespective of the personal touch, the music has survived the composer. Ladies (pause) and gentlemen, it is only, I repeat, it is only when it is in harmony with our time that music is alive and able to move us deeply. (Small outbreak of applause with a confused Levadski at its head.) And I am most decisively saying this aloud to all the academic classicists!"

"Bravo!" the great-aunts shouted. It was not in the hall, but during the intermissions, when speeches like this were bandied about, that they truly seemed to come alive.

"In the time of our grandfathers, everything was played according to their own perception of it," a heavily powdered beauty from times gone by announced. "The adaptation by a virtuoso was considered more significant that the original score!" Levadski's great-aunts nodded, gazing into the distance with nostalgia.

"And then our grandfathers died, and our fathers suddenly stood there lost," said her grace, waving her bony arms. "As if burdened by a curse, people started to play in a historically faithful manner – the slightest whim of the composer, however absurd, was maintained, even transcription errors in the first edition were celebrated as being ingenious and accepted!"

"God forbid," the great-aunts murmured, and Levadski was on the verge of making the sign of the cross. The caviar canapé tasted good because it looked like a glade filled with enlarged bark beetle eggs.

"Perfection became an obsession," the old lady whispered, lowering her eyes. "No faith was placed in chance, in a person's own nature ..."

"And music itself," groaned the great-aunts, "as fleeting and unique as it is! A spider's web in flight!" And then slightly tearfully to Levadski, "Although it is only possible to harness the music if you let it fly!"

"Our grandfathers were still able to do that," the powdered lady sighed at the stuccoed ceiling of the buffet hall, "then our fathers were conceived."

"I remember," one of the great-aunts recollected, "my

– our – father, praising an interpreter by calling his style harsh!"

"Delightful!" her sister said, pinching Levadski's hollow cheek, "now everything has changed!"

At another table a conversation was going on about the interpreter's behavior towards the composer's authority. "Passive recipient or generous servant of the composer – that is the question!"

"Willing servant, no question, willing servant!"

The ladies smiled into their glasses, as if they hoped to find a witty turn of phrase at the bottom. The gentlemen, on the other hand, dished them out and drank to the bottom. People patted each other on the padded shoulders of their tailcoats, raising particles of dust that glowed gold in the light of the crystal chandeliers.

A gentleman with sideburns and a red face, leaning on a bistro table, declared: "Not every grand piano and pianist can do justice to the Hammerklavier Sonata, Opus 106! (Inquisitive raising of plucked eyebrows.) Let us consider the well-known moment before the entrance of the reprise of the first movement!"

"Oh yes!" a blushing Fräulein in respectable schoolteacher-blue interjected. "Beethoven's Érard grand piano has very little in common with the tone and variety of our grand pianos."

"The sound of the orchestra of his time," a richly bejeweled matron with an unhealthy palor growled, "can hardly be compared to that of today, either."

"An Érard grand piano and a Steinweg! Ha!" laughed a bent old little lady with a diamond tiara, "chicken broth and goulash soup!"

"I have a fortepiano at home that is in sore need of attention at the moment," a faded diva remarked. "Its tone is like a cembalo, I should add ..."

"Oh, if you could just play a musical instrument with a

sense of humor," interrupted a corpulent woman of indeterminate age, "you only need think of Beethoven's *Kind, willst du ruhig schlafen!* It's hilarious!" (Long thoughtful pause, disappearance of the fat lady behind a curtain.)

"Well," the gentleman with the sideburns said, enlivened, "to speak of an amusing experience, I once attended a concert in a small castle during which a virtuoso interrupted his playing to throw two groaning pieces of firewood out into the snow. He killed two birds with one stone: the terrible racket in the fireplace and the coachman who was unfortunate enough to be doing his business beneath the very castle window."

One of Levadski's great-aunts was the first to disengage herself from the general state of shock. "What annoys me most are the lower middle classes in the hall who, in the silence of the general pause before the minuet, slide around on their chairs, cough and clean their pince-nez, totally oblivious to the reason why there is a general pause … (Waiting, a concerned glance towards Levadski.) What for? In order to create a state of motionless silence (a finger solemnly raised along with lacquered red fingernail), before the minuet deliciously and consolingly pours forth over the great lament."

"How anybody can be that unreceptive to music!" outraged, giving a curt nod in the direction of where the lower middle classes were mingling. "How should they know that the silence that follows the final chord is more important than the sound that goes before it? Instead of celebrating the silence for a while, they race each other to the cloakroom."

"It would be best if people like that didn't turn up here in the first place," the man with the sideburns suggested.

"That lot," laughed the fat lady who had reappeared, "can't even tell the difference between Beethoven's *pianissimo misterioso* and *dolce*!"

"What *is* the difference?" the man with the sideburns asked innocently.

"You are having me on, my dear sir," the fat woman smiled. "*Dolce* is warm gentleness. *Pianissimo misterioso* is a shudder of amazement. Oh, if I only think of the teasing finale of his variations!" she chirped, "of the sweeping polonaise, of the impetuous *Rondo alla ingharese* ..."

"Warm gentleness and a shudder of amazement," the man with the whiskers repeated thoughtfully, "I would like to be drinking what you are!"

"Wasn't that amusing?" the sisters sighed on the way to the organ balcony. "What could be more intellectually stimulating than company like that!"

At the bottom of his heart Levadski felt pity for his great-aunts. Years later, however, it was driven out by understanding and deep sympathy. The pathetic sparkle and the paltry entertainment to which the old women desperately clung could be likened to a sparsely populated lake, where a mollusk counts as half a fish. In spite of everything, it had been intellectually stimulating company, Levadski realized when he was older, intellectually stimulating by virtue of the presence of the music itself.

V

MORE AND MORE FREQUENTLY LEVADSKI'S MOTHER SPOKE of her yearning for honest country air, which in her opinion only still existed in Galicia. "Galicia just happens to be in Poland," she said, "and the war has been over for years." What spoke most in favor of a return was that Levadski had long since reached school age. "We are going back," she announced to her aunts one evening in spring. With a bow and a kiss of the hand Levadski said farewell to the old ladies. When he turned around again on the stairs to wave, he saw that the sisters had already closed the French doors. He imagined hearing heartrending sobbing behind them, a dull thud, as if a heavy velvet curtain along with the iron curtain rod itself had fallen to the ground.

At the age of eight, Levadski was sent to school in his homeland, which now belonged to the Second Polish Republic. In honor of this day a tough goose from the market was slaughtered and a broth made from its bones. Levadski made a pipe out of its gristly throat. Every morning, on Saturdays too, Levadski carted his heavy bag to school – which consisted of a single room – in the neighboring village. He had to learn Polish, which he did not find difficult as the son of a Little Russian.

Who Is Martha?

"Be happy," his mother said cheerfully, "be happy, my son, for the more languages you speak, the more human you will be!" The language of birds would have sufficed for Levadski. Even as an elementary school pupil he could have sworn that the language of birds was universal, that the only difference lay in the voices of the respective birds, and that the magpie could understand the crow, just as the blackbird could understand the duck. "What about ducks who live in a different country?" Levadski's mother asked provocatively.

"When they meet they will talk to each other in such a way that everyone understands," Levadski said. "Human beings should also find a common language. After all, we are animals too."

"That is the way it once was," said Levadski's mother. "Your father and I lived in a world like that. We had subscriptions to all sorts of bird journals: Cabanis' *Journal of Ornithology*, the *Zoological Garden*, the *Journal of the Zoological Botanical Society of Vienna*, Nitzsche's *Illustrated Hunting Journal*, bird conservation papers, and many others. They were all sent to us by post. We shopped at the Polish market, went to the Russian saddler, the local Jew sewed my wedding dress for me. Everything worked fine. The world was connected through trade, it was an aviary with the most diverse birds, who admired and enriched each other. We could send letters to all the countries of the globe, even to the director of the Caucasian Museum in Tiflis who was a bird lover and, moreover, a Prussian."

"What is a Prussian?"

"A Prussian is also a human being!" Levadski's mother laughed.

And so, time passed. While Levadski's behind was parked on the school bench in Lemberg and he ripped one pair of trousers after the other, his mother remained in the forester's hut, planted a vegetable garden and learned

Polish, so that she could subscribe to a handful of bird magazines and read them in the native tongue of the land of which she was now a citizen.

When Levadski was in his fourth year of study and poring over his thesis concerning the numerical deficiency of Corvidae, his mother sensed that something was about to happen in the world. "A Flood is nearly upon us!" she wrote to the student Levadski at the Institute of Zoology in Lemberg.

> *My Dear Son,*
>
> *Far be it from me to waste the valuable time of a future scholar with complaints that you seldom write home. The reason why your old mother has reached for her pen is an entirely different one. I ask you to open your eyes, ears and your good little heart now and acknowledge the contents of this letter in all seriousness.*
>
> *My son, something is brewing in this world. The non-migratory birds like the crested lark, wren and the common treecreeper have turned their backs on our little place, the forest and the fields. There is no sign of the house martin either. House sparrows are now nesting under the eaves. I can no longer remember the last time I saw a house martin standing before a puddle, stuffing mud into its cheeks as building material for its nest, it was such a long time ago.*
>
> *All these signs, my son, as you yourself know, are alarming. Our dear father would have said: the rats are leaving the sinking ship. He would have been right.*
>
> *For months I have been dreaming the same dream almost every night. A green woodpecker is building its breeding nest in our china cupboard. In my dream I*

know this is a great honor and fortune, but I am not happy about the visitor. I am worried about our best stoneware dinner service that has outlived your father, the decline of the monarchy and four years of war, even our three-year absence. I think about this and feel rotten – a green woodpecker is nesting beneath our roof and I am thinking of the wretched dinner service and unable to enjoy the important guest! From time to time I hear the laughter of the bird from the china cupboard, which sounds like gluckgluckgluck. Sometimes I see the long woodpecker's tongue, darting back and forth through the keyhole. It is sticky and encrusted with the crumbs of white stoneware.

This dream doesn't bode well either. A Flood is nearly upon us. This is clear to me, and it should be clear to you, too. What I would like is for you to drop everything and come home straight away. Your old mother will deal with the rest. If you pronounce me mad and don't take this letter seriously, I will, as God is my witness, follow in your father's footsteps.

Levadski read the letter, put it down on the bed and scratched his neck with both hands. A strange woman. He picked up the letter again and read it once more. "My Dear Son, Far be it from me ..."

"Damn it!" Levadski swore at the paper-thin wall, where an old photograph and a sketch depicting two rheumatic lumberjacks bowing to each other were hanging. He got up and straightened the frames. In the photograph, Levadski's father sat on the box of a carriage, with a full head of hair and no beard. A shaggy dog of indeterminate breed was sleeping on his lap. Levadski's mother was resting her beautiful head on his right arm. The sketch depicted a cuckoo perched on a rustic wooden table with an egg in its open beak, set against the backdrop of an enchanted rococo scene, a wildly overgrown arbor, a swing and thunderclouds in the distance. At the bottom right stood the year of Levadski's birth beside his father's signature: *Landscape with cuckoo, nothing special, but with the deepest affection for my little dove. Your little dove forever.*

Levadski straightened the pictures again and took a step back. "No," he said, taking the pictures off the wall and placing them in the open jaws of his suitcase. He also packed his best Sunday shirt and the folder with his thesis concerning the numerical deficiency of Corvidae.

When he was already seated in the third class carriage between clucking sacks of hens and little old sleeping grannies, he remembered he had forgotten to register for the approaching banding of the kingfishers in the Carpathians. "Never mind," Levadski sighed, closed his eyes and, insofar as the hard backrest of his seat would permit, drifted into the memory of the last banding of this magnificent bird he had been allowed to participate in. He thought of the outstretched invisibly thin net and how he touched the trembling animal for the first time. In that moment, the bird was a single heartbeat. Levadski smiled in his half sleep. After banding, the bird was completely tame and sat pensively for a while on the back of his hand. Months later a bird like this would be captured by an Egyptian colleague or found dead. Thanks to the band number it was known that kingfishers from the Carpathians flew over Turkey to the brackish water of Lake Burullus in the northerly Nile Delta, to spend the winter there. This is what they did, had done since the last ice age, and would continue doing, until something intervened.

The sack beside Levadski's left leg started to crow. Without opening her eyes, the little old granny opposite him gave the sack a kick. Something made Levadski think he would miss this year's banding of the birds.

With pins and needles in his legs, Levadski stepped off the train. On the deserted platform two male dogs were fighting in a puddle. As Levadski passed, they sprayed him with dirt and bombarded him with abuse; in his imagination, with words of an obscene nature.

To his great surprise, the village road was paved. There was a tree missing in front of the forester's house. Whether it had been a nut, an apple, or a plum tree, Levadski could no longer remember, no matter how hard he tried. At one of the windows sat his mother, wrapped in a white lace curtain like a bride, almost exactly as he had left her a year ago. The house seemed to have shrunk since then and grown into the earth. Or was his mother sitting on a stool to make the wait more comfortable?

Inside the house it smelled of onion tart, Levadski's favorite dish. The crumbs in the corner of his mother's mouth fell to the ground the second she smiled at him. Whistling, Levadski washed his hands in a bowl. He dried himself on an elaborately embroidered towel and wondered why his mother had put out one of her wedding linens. She had never before made everyday use of anything from her dowry. Hidden in a heavy wooden chest, she had saved the treasures for an uncertain future and spread them out on the lawn every few years to bleach them. And now?

Levadski stared in dismay at the brown imprint of his hands on the old linen. "It doesn't matter," his mother murmured cheerfully, "that's what it's there for!" Levadski felt a shiver run down his spine.

While he ate the onion tart he noticed a small suitcase leaning against his own near the coat rack. Levadski had great trouble swallowing his mouthful of tart. "What is that?" he said, pointing at the coat tree.

"Our suitcases," said Levadski's mother, wetting a fingertip and gathering two crumbs from the table that had fallen off Levadski's plate.

"You are like the green woodpecker from your dream," Levadski tried joking. Both gave a forced laugh.

"Yes, I have been having bad dreams lately, but they are exciting," Levadski's mother said. "I am glad you took your old mother's letter seriously. And why did you?"

Levadski shrugged his shoulders. In his head the sentences were all muddled: I have always taken you seriously, mother. The image of you rotting away for months in the forest would interfere with the writing of my thesis. The disappearance of the house martins is an ominous sign ...

"Why not?" Levadski said dryly. The onion tart sat like a stone in his stomach. He waited without looking at his mother for her to start talking.

"My dear child, your father was a wonderful man. We got to know each other in the woods where you were born and grew up. He never left these woods for as long as he lived. Don't think it is easy for me to leave them. I came here as a student from Vienna, together with three young professors, for the East Galician bird census a few years before your birth. The old count, for whom your father worked as a forest warden, was a great bird fanatic. You already know this. During the breeding season his manor house and his estates were always open to bird lovers – this was known throughout Vienna, Berlin, Paris and London. Even two nephews of the Tsar, may they rest in peace, regularly came to visit. Your father came to collect us from the railway station in a carriage. He loaded up our suitcases with such a scornful expression on his face that I nearly peed in my pants with laughter – I was one of the few women who wore them in the empire. Don't ask me why. In spite of this, your father fell in love with me. And your father won my heart completely when a bird alighted in the branches of a birch in front of our

Who Is Martha?

window. It was a common blackbird, we were a couple, I no longer wore trousers, but dresses, though in that moment I was naked, so was your dear father, by the way. You don't need to scratch your neck now. Well, when the bird alighted on the birch and obliged us with its territorial song, your father froze. He lay on top of me, listening to the bird, without blinking. He listened to the blackbird he couldn't see. He listened so intently he held his breath. And when I noticed, there was no turning back."

Levadski could have sworn he had turned into a lump of coal. For a few seconds. Then, after a conscientious clearing of his throat, he was himself again. "When you told me you wanted to study ornithology in Lemberg, you made an old widow smile for the first time in ages," Levadski's mother continued. "My heart smiled like it did long ago, when your father held his breath at the song of a common blackbird. With my heart smiling, my son, I breathed a sigh of relief for the first time since his death. Do you remember, I asked you how seriously you would take your studies in the capital city with its pernicious charms and influences? I did not mention our financial situation, it would have been unnecessary, you already knew how miserable it was. You said: Mother, I take the matter very seriously. Do you remember? It was then that it became clear to me I would without a moment's hesitation slave away for you like a cart-horse until my last drop of blood was spent. Oh, no matter what, I would have made your studies possible. What else can a mother do? My son, you made me happy back then, and now you have made me happy by coming here. Believe me, if you had not humored me, it all would have been for nothing, the life and death of your father, my life and death, the colorful dances of our ancestors, and your own life would have become a ghost ship. Believe your old mother. I, too, am taking the matter seriously."

Levadski was glad he was sitting. Sweat was pouring down his back in icy streams. "Forgive me," he said spitting out onto the plate the onion tart he had chewed to a pulp. "I can't swallow," Levadski moaned, wiping his mouth with a shaky hand. The more desperately he tried to remember the act of swallowing, the more unnatural it became.

Levadski's mother drummed her fingers on the table and continued: "A catastrophe is on its way. The starlings and sparrows have disappeared from the surrounding villages, my son. And probably from the big cities as well, from Tarnopol, Stanislau, far away Cracow. Did you notice anything in Lemberg?"

"I can't swallow any more!" Levadski sobbed.

"Then you will have to starve!" Levadski's mother's gaze drilled a hole in the plate with the spit-out puddle of pulp. Whether she was angry or deeply offended, Levadski could not say. His sudden inability to perform a basic reflex and this conversation that spelled disaster paralyzed him.

After an agonizing pause, she continued in a quiet voice:

"We need to get out of here."

"Why?" Levadski asked.

"Because the Flood is coming," his mother whispered, pouring him some tea. Levadski drank, and just as he realized that he'd managed to swallow without effort, his mother resumed talking.

"Where to, you probably want to ask. I am going to tell you what you already know. No, I won't tell you. You can guess. So, where to, where is it that we are going to escape to, to get away from the Flood? What does history teach us?"

"You mean the fairytale from the Old Testament?"

"My son," Levadski's mother said, clearing her throat

and smoothing down the invisible creases of her apron, "you may have grown up in a forester's hut, but in an educated household nevertheless. If you are going to claim that the fairytales, myths, legends and sagas that have been painstakingly passed on from one generation to the next have nothing to do with reality, you are spitting in your old mother's face."

"That's not what I'm saying, but Mo—"

"No buts! If you're not familiar with the name Noah, think of the weaver birds in Africa. You will know them. The weavers that habitually build their nests on the riverbank sense the rain a year ahead and plan accordingly in case the river swells. If a nest is hanging high up in a tree there will be a lot of rain that year. It's similar in the case of swallows in Japan who usually build their nests above ground level. If a typhoon year threatens flooding, they build their nests as high as they can. We too are going to move our nest to the hills. We are going to do the same as the birds. My suitcase is packed."

"To which mountains?" Levadski groaned.

"The high mountains, my dear son."

"I realize you are homesick and want to go skiing in the Alps," Levadski laughed. His mother had gone crazy, there was no doubt about it. "The starlings and sparrows have disappeared, you say?"

"Great titmice, blue tits and coal tits and the ancient colony of jackdaws from the village church," his mother said, listing them.

"I understand, I understand," Levadski mumbled, "so where is the journey taking us?"

"To the Caucasus." Levadski's eyes widened. "You were thinking Mount Ararat? Your mother isn't Noah. That would be uninspired. Have you ever heard of Chechnya?"

Levadski frowned. North Caucasus. Nothing came to

mind apart from the fact that the Caucasian goldcrest was to be found there 6,500 feet above sea level, and that it was said to be lighter than the Central European goldcrest. An elegant bird with orange colored head feathers it would impressively raise when rankled.

"Sisisisisisi … ," Levadski sang gently, as if to entice the bird from the scent of the onion tart.

"Sisisi-sia!" his mother chimed in. "Everything will turn out fine," she said, placing her hand on Levadski's shoulder.

Everything would be fine, is what Levadski wanted to say and burst into tears. But he didn't move. He felt like a pillar in the ruins of a palace, a pillar on which a goldcrest sits, striking up a song.

"The Caucasian goldcrest is all you can think of? God in Heaven, what have you been doing at university in Lemberg?" Levadski's mother got up from the chair. From below, she looked like she had silently and secretly died during Levadski's absence. Levadski also rose and went to the window. His mother turned towards him. What a relief! From this angle she looked like an old woman, a faded beauty, blossoming decay, a firm figure of resolution.

"The red-necked goose, my son. Branta ruficollis. The favorite dish of the Caucasus. Did you not come across it in your studies?"

"We mainly explored the birds of Europe."

"Dear child. Don't you have any world maps, eyes in your head? Chechnya is in the North Caucasus and therefore in Europe. Wake up!"

"Who says so?" Levadski laughed.

"I do, and so does science."

"What science?" Levadski shook with laughter. Tears rolled down his face. Or were they beads of sweat?

"Don't cry," said Levadski's mother. Levadski made a dismissive gesture and howled. "Cartography, geography and human intelligence tell us so, my son," she went on. "The Caucasus lies on the edge of Europe, and with that, Elbrus is our highest mountain."

The northern red-necked goose, the most colorful and beautiful of all the sea geese, really had flown past Levadski the student without making a noise. How could he live, learn, drink honey vodka, without knowing that the red-neck goose existed, that it bred in the tundra of West Siberia and wintered on the southwest coast of the Caspian Sea? It was a mystery to him.

"Is it really such a magnificent bird, the northern red-necked goose?" Levadski asked with a tear-stained face.

"Yes," said his mother and handed him her handkerchief embroidered with calyces set in squares.

"If they arrive in great droves at the Caspian Sea, you can definitely conclude there is a bitterly cold winter further in the north. The geese live according to a strict daily routine in their winter habitat: before sunrise they take off for the grazing land. The main swarm with thousands of birds sets out last. When the sun goes down, the return flight to their overnight stay begins." Levadski let the tears flow. "You must follow me," Levadski's mother said and shrugged her shoulders. "I am going!" she said a little louder and raised her eyebrows, throwing her forehead into a myriad of unflattering lines.

"Why are you doing this?"

"Because it must be so."

"What must be so? You must manipulate me, exploit my love for you and throw my studies to the wind? After all, you paid for them, mother!"

"That's beside the point. When my child's life is at stake, I am unwavering. You are coming with me, and if you are not, then I will go and die far away from you in an ignominious manner. And nobody will commit my body to the earth."

"This is blackmail, madness!" said Levadski stamping his foot.

"So it is," Levadski's mother said, "I am going now."

VI

LEVADSKI WENT WITH HIS MOTHER. FROM A FLY-INFESTED train station in southern Russia, he wired his institute in Lemberg. DETAINED STOP MOTHER ILL STOP PERMISSION FOR TIME OFF STOP

From time to time he felt a faint glimmer of hope that his mother would turn back as soon as she saw the snow-covered peaks of Mount Kazbek and drank from the pure springs, and that he would be able to continue dedicating his time to his birds and his studies, and the letter and all talk of an imminent Flood would simply be a bad dream. Levadski's mother caught sight of Mount Kazbek's peak, drank from pure springs, and did not turn back. Not in her dreams did she think of turning her back on the mountains.

They stayed the night in guesthouses with ceilings that grew lower and lower; fleas ransacked their beds. Swallow nests, at which a landlord proudly pointed a dirty finger, hung like old hamburgers from the beams of the house. When Levadski and Levadski's mother more frequently came across shepherds by the wayside leaning on their staffs and wearing tall fur hats, Levadski knew: there was no going back.

In a Chechen mountain village almost seven thousand feet above sea level, Levadski became a shepherd. His mother became the wife of the village elder and the ornament of the village, an honor she owed to her pale skin, the result of an iron deficiency. From his stepfather, Levadski received a tall sheep's wool hat that covered half his face. He wore it and looked like the other eyeless men everywhere nodding off, leaning on their staffs. Slowly Levadski embraced the hat. He believed he could think clearly beneath it. The tall fur hat wasn't completely absurd. During the day it protected Levadski's head from the heat, in the evening from the cold. Here, too, the dear Lord breathed purpose into all things that men were given to create.

After a year as a shepherd, when Levadski toyed with the idea of leaving his mother and resuming his studies, German soldiers marched into Poland. The Flood drowned the land. It drowned Lemberg. It drowned Stanislau, Tarnopol, Brody, forests and marshes, it licked the claws of the startled birds and sent its fetid breath to the stars. The stars said to hell with the Flood, just as they had always said to hell with the Flood. This in itself was a consolation. The ornithological institute in Lemberg was bound to be closed, Levadski thought, I can in all likelihood once again forget about banding the birds this year.

The Flood spread further to the east. "They won't get this far," Levadski's mother said. She was right. The Germans were stopped at Mozdok in North Ossetia and never reached Chechnya. This, however, did not prevent the Russians from cramming all the Chechens into trains and deporting them to Central Asia as traitors and collaborators with the German army.

Perhaps it was owing to Levadski's mother's dazzlingly white skin and Levadski's height (he was two heads taller than the other Chechen shepherds) that the two enjoyed the privilege of being allowed to work in a kolkhoz. Levadski's mother milked cows from dawn till dusk and mourned for her second husband, who had died on the deportation train. Levadski worked his way up from load hauler to first secretary of the kolkhoz.

Years later, everything that had legs was on the move: the Chechens went back to Chechnya, Levadski and his mother went back to the village that was now part of Ukraine. When they stepped off the train his mother suddenly stood still and gripped Levadski by the sleeve, as if she had choked on a word. Then they continued on their way.

They strode towards the village like lovers, over furrowed and frozen fields. Levadski saw the village houses leaning against each other like old acquaintances, embarrassed, as if they had been spattered with excrement. None of them had stirred from their place. The forester's house had shaken off its roof in the years of separation and filled with bitterness, and perhaps out of defiance, too, it had spit out all its doors and window frames. Blind and shattered, it crouched there beneath an open sky.

"The birdbath is missing," Levadski's mother declared and burst into tears. The count's birdbath, a present made by the old nobleman on the occasion of Levadski's birth, was gone. Levadski knew that it had arrived wrapped in gold paper and tied with a velvet bow, a present as fateful as a split second in which one looks into another's eyes before diving into a fatal passion. There was no trace of the birdbath anymore, and for a fleeting moment Levadski felt as if he had never been born, as if he had spent these years as a wandering bubble, imagining that it had all been a dream in his head. When they turned around and went back to the railway station, the strange feeling had left him.

Levadski's mother died in a drafty Lemberg hospital filled

with creaky beds, shortly after Levadski's promotion. The coughing, even the sighs of the patients, became a tragi-comic affair through the ever-present creaking. Levadski's mother laughed constantly; her bed laughed with her. She was always saying romantic things. "My heart is a broken sugar bowl, my son, your mother's teeny old heart is a teeny bone china cup." The diminutives cost her a lot of effort, but seemed to amuse her much: "In death everything becomes smaller, just as it should, my son," she said, smiling. Levadski nodded and knew that he would understand later. Much later, just not now. "So, here we are," were her last words. Levadski often thought of this, and that nothing better would have occurred to him in her place.

VII

LEVADSKI WAS SITTING IN THE KITCHEN, BLOWING ON THE flower created by the gas flame. The petals dispersed and grew back immediately. "I can also strangle you," Levadski said to the flame and switched it off. The soft hiss of the gas flower died away. "Your company bores me!" said Levadski to the stove.

With shuffling steps he entered the living room, and as he could think of nothing better to do, sat down in the rocking chair, which he instantly regretted. Getting up – wrath of the Almighty! – was getting more difficult the more years Levadski had at his back. He stared at his telephone as if wanting to hypnotize it: come here, come here, come over here! The telephone did not react. Groaning, Levadski lifted himself out of the rocking chair, went to the phone, and grabbed the receiver. As he dialed the number of his favorite radio station, he could feel his hand growing clammy. Radio World Harmony – the number he had memorized years ago and never used. Now I am ninety-six, thought Levadski, and I am calling a radio station like a schoolboy!

"Radio World Harmony" the voice answered.

"Good evening, I have a re–"

"Before we connect you with one of our staff members," the voice continued, "we would like to ask you to participate in our survey."

"A request," Levadski said a little more loudly into the receiver, "a song by Ra–"

"Please respond to the questions with yes or no," the voice said.

"–by Ray Price, *For The Good Times*," Levadski said.

"Ready! Let's begin. First question: are you listening to us over the radio?" Levadski's eyes widened.

"How else? What nonsense!"

"Sorry, your answer was unclear. Are you listening to us on the internet?"

"Oh right! No."

"Sorry, your answer was unclear. Are you a young listener?"

"No."

"Thank you for your answer. Are you satisfied with the variety of music that the station offers?"

"Yes."

"Thank you for your answer. Do you find our radio hosts pleasant and easy to listen to?"

"Well ..."

"Sorry, your answer was unclear. Would you like more features on culture?" Levadski waved his hand in the air.

"By all means, yes!"

"Sorry, your answer was unclear ..."

"My God, you stupid snail!" Levadski shouted into the receiver.

"... Thank you for participating in our survey. We are connecting you."

"Radio World Harmony. Good evening!"

"Are you there?" Levadski asked cautiously.

"Where else?" the voice said with indignation.

"Excuse me. Good evening. I have a request, a song by Ray Price – *For the Good Times*."

Who Is Martha?

"Let's see," the voice said, "Ray Price. Ray Price … *For the Good Times*. We'll play it between 10 and 11 p.m. during the request show."

"Thank you!"

"Not at all." The voice turned into a dead dial tone. Levadski placed the phone on the receiver. He waited for the request show. His song was the last.

How often, thought Levadski, have I laughed at the people who call up the radio station, and now I have done it myself! Levadski felt something akin to deep satisfaction.

Don't look so sad
I know it's over.

"Oh dear," Levadski sighed.

But life goes on
And this old world
Will keep on turning.
Let's just be glad
We had some time

"To spend together," Levadski whispered.

To spend together …
And make believe you love me
One more time
For the good times …

"… and now for the news of the day."

Levadski switched off the radio. He lay down in bed and imagined he was lying in the suite in the Hotel Imperial where he'd stayed during the Northern Bald Ibis Conference in Vienna in 2002. In the spacious room the air was heavy with the scent of flowers and furniture polish. An imposing crystal chandelier sprouted from a ceiling rose. It swung above Levadski like a cut teardrop. Back and forth, back and forth, and sleep seeps through the midnight blue silk wallpaper on the walls. Delicious silence.

The next morning Levadski dialed the number of the Konrad Lorenz Research Center. A young lady gave her double-barreled name in a singsong voice. Levadski introduced himself by reading out the captions of some newspaper articles that had been sent to him after the conference. "Foster father in a light airplane: away with the borders! Reintroduction into the wild project, historically unparalleled. Paving the way ahead, Ukrainian ornithologist breaks all barriers ... Well, yes. Barriers, barriers, barriers, you see, Madam, human beings are forever being confronted with limitations, internal or external. Sometimes the shoes are too tight, sometimes the coffin too close, do you understand what I mean?"

The employee of the Konrad Lorenz Research Center seemed to be crying in silence at the other end of the receiver, then Levadski heard an escalation of strangled sounds and asked the young lady to connect him with a man. When a male voice answered at the other end of the line, Levadski introduced himself again by reading the same captions. "Foster father in a light plane: away with the borders! Reintroduction into the wild project, historically unparalleled. Paving the way ahead, Ukrainian ornithologist breaks all barriers."

"Oh, Professor Levadski, of course, of course. The young lady? Oh, right. An intern. Yes, yes. Exactly. Overtaxed is the right word. Exactly. Our best. Exactly. But of course people still know who you are. Of course. Even small fry like myself. I have grown up with your intellectually stimulating articles in the annual magazine. Sorry? Whether I personally liked them? For example, *On the Red-Backed Shrike's Humane Art of Impaling Insects and Large Prey on Thorns*, or *How Global Warming Alters Fish Stocks and Turns North Sea Birds into Cannibals*. Sorry? You would like a favor?"

What was at stake was nothing less than the project of a lifetime, Levadski said, his last research project, and he needed an invitation from the Research Center for an express visa. As a Ukrainian it wasn't so easy to get across the border, member of the Academy of Sciences or not.

The male voice asked for Levadski's passport number and promised he would deal with everything.

After this fruitful conversation he dialed the number of the Academy of Sciences, where he was recognized by voice and put through to the director, something that always used to flatter him and to which he was now indifferent. Levadski explained the matter: he urgently had to get to Vienna. He was ninety-six and didn't have time to detain himself with paperwork. What he expected from the Academy was for them to call the embassy and speak to the director of the visa department and persuade them that he was a special case. He entreated them to do so. If informed that no exceptions could be made, they were immediately to go on the attack and make use of his membership in the Academy of Sciences and his doctorate and honorary degrees.

Levadski received his visa within two weeks. When he turned the key in the lock, a thin leather suitcase between his legs, it was as if the rumbling in his stomach was calling out to the silence in his apartment. "I am not coming back," he said to the oval porcelain plaque with the number 107 on his door. With a bad conscience he got into the elevator. He was leaving his home like a wife he never had. He turned his back on his apartment, his apartment that welcomed him on a daily basis, warmed him, embraced him. True, he'd had to cook himself, but the apartment was there for him and surrounded him day and night, in silent selfless love. My God, Levadski thought, what has become of me? A traitor! An egotist! By the time he stepped out of the elevator Levadski couldn't care less about his egotism.

In the taxi, he inspected the visa in his passport with a magnifying glass. It loomed even larger in size than the one he had been given in 2002. Security precautions, thought Levadski, are getting tighter.

"Traffic jam," said the taxi driver. Levadski was happy that, as was his habit, he had set off far too early. He was happy about his hat and his walking stick, leaning against his thin leg like a gaunt grayhound. In order not to look out the taxi window, and to avoid becoming unnecessarily melancholy, Levadski opened his wallet. A beautiful credit card beamed at him like an oriental beauty through the slit of her veil. What a kerfuffle over such a small item! Levadski thought. Luckily, it had been sorted quickly. Levadski had only applied for the credit card the previous week. He received it shortly after the courier had arrived with his passport and visa. Let them say what they like about bureaucracy!

"We are on the move," the taxi driver announced ceremoniously. "An accident with a few fatalities."

"Wonderful," Levadski said and started counting the knuckles on his hand with the handle of the drinking stick; he counted them clockwise and counter-clockwise. He continued to count them until they passed the spot of the accident.

At the airport the crowd took no notice of Levadski's smart outward appearance or his considerable age. For the last time, he thought, and dived into the swathes of people who smelled of sweat, perfume and onions. Half an hour later, Levadski was washed up on the banks of passport and customs control. His drinking stick got through the checkpoint without causing a stir. Levadski followed suit. My God, he thought, sitting on one of the hard metal benches in front of the departure gate, One way, and no coming back! To calm himself he unscrewed his drinking stick, threw his head back and drank the contents of the glass tube: Cognac. Make: 3 Star Odessa Cognac. For the last time, Levadski thought, a native comestible.

"What's that?" a child who'd appeared out of nowhere asked.

"A drinking stick, my dear boy," Levadski replied.

"I am not a boy," the child growled. "Where did you get the stick?"

"In a shop at 5 Victory Avenue. Do you like it?"

"No. But my father does," said the child and pointed at one of the customs officers standing with his legs spread apart, who, so it seemed to Levadski, was winking at him in a friendly manner with the muzzle of his gun.

VIII

On November 6, 2010, Levadski landed in Vienna. It was a Saturday and shortly after four. "Hotel Imperial please," he said in a cracked voice to the broad, cobra-like back of the taxi driver.

"Oh, Imperial," said the taxi driver, his leather jacket squeaking. "You know it's the best hotel in town?"

"I know," Levadski said and felt his heart pounding at the portals of his brain.

"How long are you staying there?"

"I don't know."

"You can speak our language very well!" This praise coming from the mouth of a pitch-black man made Levadski laugh. "Where are you from?" he asked Levadski with a heavy accent.

"I'm from the East." Levadski paused. "From Ukraine." He noticed he was lying. He was lying, even though he was telling the truth. In the political sense Levadski really was from Ukraine, it was written in black and white in his passport, but from a historical perspective he was from two utopias: Austro-Hungary and the Soviet Union. The one and only thing that smacked of a lie was the realization that Levadski had survived two systems of government.

"I know Ukraine," said the taxi driver, "I studied tele-communications in Germany, my roommate was from Kiev. His name was Petro and he always ate sour pickles in the morning to get his hangover under control. He liked to joke. For example, when I scratched my head, he would say: 'Don't scratch – wash!'" Levadski broke into a dirty laugh and immediately apologized. "Yes, Petro was funny …"

"Are you still in touch with him?"

The taxi driver shook his head. His black face had a purple sheen to it in the red of the traffic light. "He's dead. Froze to death on a park bench in winter."

"Oh," said Levadski.

"Yes," said the taxi driver. "That wouldn't have happened to him in the Ivory Coast. That's where I'm from."

With every new traffic light, Levadski warmed a little more to the taxi driver. He would have liked to examine him by daylight. "What do you think of our language?" the taxi driver asked him.

"Which language?"

"The German language," the taxi driver laughed. Beautiful. Levadski thought it was a very beautiful language, and romantic. The taxi driver cautiously turned round, his leather jacket scrunching madly. "You know, this is the first time I am hearing someone say that German is a beautiful language. I am pleased, because I think it is too."

"I am pleased to hear it," Levadski said. He would have liked to continue talking about the beauty of the German language but didn't say anything. He remained silent and took pleasure in the rising bubbles of joy, savored the experience of sitting beneath the roof of a car with a special person, a black taxi driver, Ivorian by birth, someone who had studied telecommunications, who had borrowed the German language. Levadski smiled in the darkness of the taxi.

"What do you think of the EU?" the man from the Ivory Coast wanted to know.

"The EU is a blessing. Migratory birds, for example, have always been real Europeans."

"That's terrific," said the taxi driver. "Terrific," he repeated softly, as if a state secret had just been entrusted to him and he had understood its meaning.

Levadski's drinking cane exited the taxi like a gentle hoof, followed by a slightly clumsier Levadski. A liveried bellhop disappeared through a side door with his suitcase. "Goodbye!" Levadski waved to the taxi driver. A chain of fireflies lit up the darkness of the car's interior.

"Take care!" the taxi driver shouted, "Long live the birds!" Smiling, Levadski stepped from the revolving door into the hotel lobby.

"A reservation has been made for me. Levadski is my name. Luka Levadski."

Shortly after the liveried bellhop deposited Levadski's suitcase with a dull thud on the luggage rack and took his leave with the intimation of a bow, there was a soft and melodious ringing at the door. Before Levadski could even say "Come in," a petite chambermaid wearing a white cap, whom Levadski guessed might have been Spanish or Portuguese, entered. She approached Levadski, whose attempt to get up out of the deep rococo armchair remained fruitless. When she noticed his arduous swinging back and forth, she hastened her step in an attempt to prevent Levadski from rising. She opened out her palms like headlights as she came towards him. She had only come to ask whether everything was to his satisfaction. Levadski nodded, perfectly content.

"If you would like the sheets changed, just throw the card on the bed. Card on bed – change. Card not on bed –

Who Is Martha?

don't change," the chambermaid explained and held up a gray postcard. Levadski watched her throw the card onto the bed twice and pick it up from the bedspread again. While throwing, she raised one eyebrow and then let her hand drop casually. It was really just a single dropping of a card from the hand of a person who was used to being served. When she picked up the card it bowed to her like to someone held in high estimation, a completely flat and square person.

"I have got it," Levadski said, when the chambermaid wanted to repeat the procedure once more. How long would he be staying, she wanted to know. "I don't know," Levadski said, "hopefully long enough." The chambermaid gave a conspiratorial smile. The Elisabeth Suite was just the right ticket for an old man like himself, in her opinion.

"I know this suite," he said, "You must excuse me for remaining seated." He would offend her if he were to get up now, the chambermaid said. "As a gentleman I find it much more difficult to remain seated in front of a lady than to get up," Levadski admitted.

"I don't understand," the chambermaid said smiling and blushed.

"I know this room," Levadski repeated, "I have stayed here once before. As an official speaker at a conference for birds. It is the same room, with the midnight blue silk wallpaper, the magnificent Louis XVI furniture, the crystal chandeliers, mirrored doors and the bathroom with a gilded domed ceiling. It can only be the same room."

A classic room wouldn't be the right choice for you, the chambermaid said. Not so big. The bathroom too small. Only a shower. It was only here that he would be able to let off steam. Levadski laughed. "If I could, yes!" The chambermaid shook her head slightly at a loss and made her way towards the door. There was pride in her gait, resolve and character. Levadski liked it. "That's the way a thresher crosses a field," he thought, "thrusting her legs like tired whips."

When the door had closed and the rattling of the keys at the chambermaid's hips was no longer audible, Levadski rose groaning from his armchair and picked up the gray card from the bed. "With pleasure," it read, "we will service your room every day. We are happy to change your sheets if you place this gray card on the bed." Levadski let the card drop as instructed and picked it up again. "A shame to die," he sighed, "things are only just beginning to get exciting."

He entered the bathroom, which was about the same size as his apartment on Veteran Street. The State can have the apartment, Levadski thought, I am going to sit in this bath until doomsday, I have no other choice! I won't for the life of me be able to get out of it by myself! Levadski desperately wanted to take a bath. With a tub like this it would be a sin not to bathe!

May the sun go down, but let me have my bath! He was choked by sadness. His old moldy bath suddenly appeared before him, dumb and unreproachful. It had been an evening like every other, Levadski had returned from his customary constitutional, made himself a fried egg, sat down in his rocking chair, leafed through a paper on *Pedantic Waste Disposal and Its Influence on the Diet of Birds of Prey*, yawned, stood up, shuffled into the bathroom and turned on the bath. Then he changed his mind and pulled the drain plug. A shower would be enough. An evening like any other. But something was not right. On this evening Levadski lost interest in climbing into his bath for the simple reason that he didn't like it anymore. He didn't like it anymore because it had grown old, through no fault of its own. It had aged, had been cleaned less and less by its master and had acquired deep scratches. "I haven't taken a bubble bath for years," Levadski thought. One thing was certain: if his old bath could see *this* one, it would crack with grief.

"I want to take a bath," he pleaded into the receiver of the telephone that hung on the wall of the bathroom.

"The gentleman would like to take a bath," the concierge ascertained, full of sympathy.

"I would like a strong, preferably short-sighted hotel employee," Levadski added bashfully, "somebody who can pull me out of the bathtub after bathing."

"I will send someone who wears glasses to your room," the concierge whispered. Levadski thanked him and hung up.

A sturdy young man with dark rings under his eyes that were visible from a distance and a ridiculous cap on his round head entered the room. The proud name of the hotel and *Vienna* glittered in gold italics on his cap. Like an embarrassed circus bear, hands folded as if in prayer, he headed towards Levadski.

"Butler service, good day," the young man said when he came to a stop in front of Levadski.

"Do you know what the most beautiful thing about this suite is apart from the bathroom?" Levadski asked, and gave the answer himself. "The ring of the doorbell. What a melody! It is not at all quiet but is nevertheless pleasant."

The butler, whose cradle, Levadski conjectured, must have stood in a sand-whipped oriental oasis, gave him a big-toothed smile. The name Habib was engraved on the shiny name badge on his chest. Habib looked at Levadski attentively, the way you do when you are unsure of whether people are listening to you with interest or just counting the lines in the face opposite them.

"I wear contact lenses. You wanted somebody shortsighted."

"I wanted to take a bath," Levadski said, "but I am no longer able to climb out of the tub on my own. If you would be so kind as to help me out when I am done, and turn a blind eye." The butler was astonished.

"Blind an eye when I pull you out of the water?"

"Just look away," Levadski laughed. The butler understood. He too would be old one day, nobody could dodge fate.

Several times Levadski invited the butler to take a seat while he lay in the bath, but he literally stood his ground. One may not sit in front of guests. Levadski tried arguing that he could not comfortably splash around in the water knowing that someone was standing behind him. Habib agreed to sit on the pouf and wait. "Why not in the armchair or on the beautiful six-legged sofa?" The butler assured him that he did not need a backrest in order to sit comfortably.

In the bathtub Levadski contemplated sitting comfortably. You needed a backrest. No question. You get a backache without a backrest. But who knows, perhaps keeping up appearances is the only sensible kind of comfort. We decide to feel comfortable, a lot more comfortable than we would in a misshapen orthopedically optimized piece of furniture.

"Do you like Beethoven?" the butler's voice penetrated his sleep. Levadski gave a start and put a wet hand to his chest. Every time he thought his dentures had gone astray he had to touch his chest.

"Yes," he called back hoarsely. Why was he asking? Breathing heavily, Levadski recovered from his fright, and already the sound of the first bars of Symphony No. 9 in D-Minor, Op. 125 filled the room. Written in the years when Beethoven was already completely deaf. Lonely and estranged from everyone, thought Levadski, feeling an icicle pierce the muscle of his heart. His last symphony

... *Freude schöner Götterfunken*, Joy, beautiful spark of divinity, la la la lalalala! Somewhere, Levadski had read, there were hundreds of Beethoven's conversation books. The deaf man got by in everyday life, armed with a pencil and a notebook. Better than nothing. That the need to communicate with people never seems to have diminished for Beethoven! People are people, thought Levadski, paddling in the water, music really must be inside us, but not being able to hear any birds – that must be difficult. Levadski closed his eyes and stopped paddling. The forest of violins advanced into the bathroom, beseeching flutes circled around the crystal chandelier for several chords, and then fate violently began to trample. And again the rustling of the violins like leaves in the whistling wind of the flutes. If a resident orchestra is part of the butler service, then I really am lost for words, thought Levadski.

"Where is the music coming from?" he called out during a quiet moment, in the direction of the door.

"From the CD player!" the butler answered. His voice sounded soft, almost like Red Riding Hood in a forest of violins.

After the uplifting *Molto vivace* Levadski asked the butler to pull him out of the water. The young man didn't seem to be doing it for the first time. "Are there many guests in the hotel who require assistance when they are bathing?" Levadski wanted to know.

"They sometimes do. The butlers are here to cater to people's special needs, and besides I have a father," said Habib. "Had," he added. "In broad daylight a strangeness suddenly overcame him and he collapsed in the middle of the room. He lay on the carpet gasping; a stroke. I looked after him until he died. Then I came here and became a hotel bellboy and later a butler."

Levadski would have liked to say something fortifying.

Breathing laboriously, wrapped in a dressing gown, he sat on the edge of the bed and looked at the shiny badge on Habib's chest. "Your name is Habib," Levadski said with the slight hint of a question. Habib demonstrated his affirmation by doubling his chin.

Screeching, a streetcar turned into the Kärnter Ring Boulevard. "I am tired," said Levadski, "I would like to sleep now." Habib removed himself. His steps were as contained as those of the chambermaid. Both belonged entirely to the rolling fire-red carpet, to the white doors and gold-plated door handles. Both allowed this confident proud knowledge to flow into their limbs and into the strength of their movements. Habib turned again at the threshold and carefully pulled the door closed behind him, as if he imagined that Levadski had already fallen asleep while he'd been sitting there. I will never forget it, thought Levadski, never.

IX

LEVADSKI DID NOT HAVE MUCH TIME LEFT TO FORGET.
According to the diagnosis he should have felt dreadful.
Considerable loss of weight, night sweats, fever, faintness
– but apart from palpitations that gripped Levadski as if
he was a youngster when he moved from window to window in his Elisabeth Suite or admired the array of orna-
ments in the room, all these symptoms were kept waiting.
From the breast pocket of his pajamas, however, his heart
announced an overwhelming joy at beautiful things, pleasure and desire, to see beauty like the light of God's face.
Beauty in spite of the revolting decay of the institution of
his body, beauty in spite of ugliness and precisely because
of it. Beauty.

Levadski stepped to the window. On the opposite
side of the street the comforting *Phoenix Pharmacy* sign
glowed above the archways of a building. And beneath it,
in small unassuming lettering: *since 1870.* Two streetcars
drove past each other. Levadski looked at the streetcars
that blocked his view of the pharmacy. The driver who
sported an imposing potbelly appeared to be dozing in
the darkness of his cabin. *Catch the Beat. House of Music*
was written on the white roof of the streetcar.

The other streetcar stopped immediately in front of

Levadski's window. It was of modern construction, black-red-gray-dark gray, the interior glaring brightly. An old lady with a gigantic white poodle on her lap was sitting at the front, in the area for pregnant women and the disabled. The poodle, glassy eyed, stared out the window at an even whiter dog floating behind it in the form of a little cloud of smoke – a ghost, a drowned twin brother, a hushed up doggie mishap. Slowly the streetcar swam by.

Levadski winced. They weren't singed banknotes, after all, but wilted leaves which swept across the street. A white paper cup was being kicked by the wind's invisible foot. Peace, an unbelievable peace, like after a clap of thunder, suffused Levadski's slight body. Bitter and terrifying. Dizzying. A transparent onion skin in the diluted soup of Levadski's life.

I should really be feeling awful, thought Levadski, it's called a small cell bronchial carcinoma, the animal I have been bitten by. It put its whole lousy soul into the bite. In principle, an admirable and selfless deed. Levadski dropped onto his canopied bed, fell asleep and dreamed he was in a baroque church at an organ recital. The music makes him cry. He sobs like a child. Through the tears, Levadski sees how the music creates movement, how it rolls the glittering molecules of air towards the altar, like billiard balls. The golden angels whirring around the altar fall to the ground. Saint Peter, the cross in his sinewy hand, leaning over the abyss, falls in. Clouds of silver and gold come crashing down after hundreds of years. Levadski, listening to the organ, drenched in tears, is covered by a cloud of dust.

A coughing fit woke Levadski in the middle of the night. He reached for his wallet on the night table and extracted a piece of paper, the bill from the laboratory, which had arrived shortly before his departure flight. He had absolutely no intention of paying it. Beneath the stated balance, an impudent laboratory technician had permitted himself to comment on Levadski's condition: inoperable, chemotherapy and radiotherapy recommended for prolongation of life (a few months). Medication: polychemotherapy.

"Pure nonsense," Levadski scolded. He put the note back on the night table. "The stuff doesn't seem as anodyne as nonpareils." He tossed and turned in bed until dawn, anticipating the symptoms of the illness. The more he concentrated on the wet embrace of his nightshirt, the more he perspired. It's happening, thought Levadski, now I'm getting the night sweats.

A chambermaid must have rung and entered on silent paws while Levadski was shoving his ball-retained dentures into his mouth in front of the bathroom mirror, like a bread roll that was far too big. Levadski was startled and apologized for still being in his bathrobe, but he was sweating so profusely. The chambermaid reckoned this was due to the air-conditioning that was heating his room to an incredible seventy-seven degrees. She adjusted a dial on the wall. It would get cooler soon, she promised, and besides, the air-conditioning switched itself off automatically if you opened one of the windows. So, no symptoms after all, Levadski registered with disappointment.

"Where are you from?" The wiry chambermaid, who was already on her way to the door, turned around, beaming. Her hands, much too ungainly for her arms, appeared to flutter. She must be a laundry woman, thought Levadski, with hands like that. Or a gray heron. She was from the south of Serbia. Near Novi Pazar. Alarming, thought Levadski, how embarrassingly touching someone else's pleasure can be, how easy it is to awaken it! Even with a mundane question which you ask only so as not to be silent. Alarming.

"Novi Pazar is beautiful. Village too. Here my home."
The short-haired woman pulled a light pink cell phone
from her apron and after pressing several times on the
buttons, pointed at a photo, in which Levadski could see
nothing but a neglected building site in the middle of a
gentle hill surrounded by woodland.

"My heart is my house. Green," the chambermaid
smiled in the direction of Levadski's suspicious eyebrow.
"I finish build, when back. Here finish work, there finish
build. Here," with one finger, the chambermaid traced a
circle in the emptiness that lay beyond the periphery of
the picture, "sister's house. We nine children. Two sisters
dead. Here!" The chambermaid let Levadski look at a picture of two gravestones and then cheerfully clicked on. In
an overexposed photograph a boy was hugging a girl on a
children's bicycle. "Children of my brother. And here me."
In the midst of sprawling bushes Levadski recognized the
chambermaid. She was wearing a shirt covered with over-
sized raspberries. "Raspberries back there. Jam, juice, own
products, in Novi Pazar we have everything. Here letter
for you. From reception. Almost forgot. I go now."

Levadski took the letter. The simple solemnnity of the
moment drove a tear into his eye, but the remarkably firm
handshake of the chambermaid with the raspberry garden
and the unbuilt house instantly cheered him up again.

Dear Mister Levadski,

*As you made use of our butler service yesterday, we
would like to advise you that you are most welcome at
any time to avail yourself of the services of our butlers
throughout your sojourn at our hotel. If you are interested in a personal butler, please call reception.*

Levadski was chewing a banana when the telephone
rang. "Come in," Levadski called in the direction of the

door. He was annoyed that a piece of banana fell out of his mouth and onto the carpet when he did so. The telephone rang several times more before Levadski's gaze gave up on the door. Rocking and wheezing, he got to his feet, trotted over to the desk and picked up the receiver.

The concierge wished Levadski a very good morning. Levadski wished the concierge the same. He had just read the letter and would be interested in the butler from yesterday. The concierge acknowledged this wise decision with a pregnant pause. The butler service would be deducted from Levadski's credit card at the end of his stay, together with the extras, the concierge said. "What extras?" Levadski wanted to know.

"Telephone, internet, minibar, breakfast, hotel bar, restaurant, barbers," the concierge-voice rattled off.

And funeral, thought Levadski, giggling into the receiver.

"Do you see the butler button on your telephone? Above it there is a button with a picture of a man in a black bow tie with a coffee cup," the concierge said. Levadski saw it. All he had to do was press the button once and the butler would come.

"When I press the button, I would like Habib to come."

"But of course, sir. Habib will be informed immediately."

This is what things have come to, thought Levadski, an oriental youngster serving an old Ruthenian. From a Ruthenian to a Bohemian, he rhymed.

Levadski dressed himself for breakfast. Buying a new suit, along with the resolve to await death pleasurably in a grand hotel, had been one of the best ideas of his too-long life. Although, thought Levadski, it all seems to have been a little on the short side. This snippet of time I have grappled with. A tiny puddle! Levadski tied his favorite bow tie with the red-billed choughs and marveled at the strange expression. Why was he thinking about a tiny puddle? In the gigantic mirror, an elegant gnome held its silence.

On the sea I was born
On the sea I was raised;
Swore unto the sea did I
To take her as my eternal bride:
To drown therefore my lot would be
As a sailor on the sea,

sang Levadski, to himself. It was as if his life had been a dream of a future and resolute being, of an ultimately irrational being and a sophisticate, of someone whose existence had been worthwhile. And now he was perfect and his life would step outside of him and stand before him, to marvel at him: you have become useless, Levadski. Pah!

Smartly dressed and feeling slightly hungry, Levadski stepped out into the corridor. The elevator came almost immediately, opening its golden chest. From all sides Levadski could see a small bald dandy staring back at him. This hotel is a ship, thought Levadski stepping into the elevator, a ship, and I am a black-headed gull on deck.

E
AUSGANG / EXIT
HALLE / LOBBY
RESTAURANT / CAFÉ / BAR

A BLACK-HEADED GULL ON DECK. LARUS RIDIBUNDUS. Larus, Larus ... the name sounds like an invocation. I chose the suit well, true to myself ... Here I stand, my breath and I, I and my pathetic little soul. How flat the buttons with the floor numbers are! G for ground, M for Maisonette Suite and my suite, 1, 2, 3, 4, 5. A black-headed gull on deck. Poppycock, it can't be on deck. The black-headed gull can do nothing but follow a ship. It follows the giants of the ocean that slowly set out from harbor. It catches everything the sailors throw to it: flowers, potatoes, nails. It does! With the chocolate-colored hood it displays during the breeding season it can easily be distinguished from other types of gulls, assuming you know which one it is. I know which one it is. But I would, however, like to seriously question my own corporality at this moment in time. So comforting are the lights here in the golden cabin, so dull any memory of pain, so dim. I can prolong or curtail the flight at any time and enter another dimension. Go to the fifth and last floor for example. But now it is time to hover.

The elevator opens its chest. To step onto the carpet, to dip your foot noiselessly into the softness, is a revelation. Levadski's delight gives way to astonishment: in a display cabinet in front of the entrance to the café there is a gleaming black and gold lorgnette with an elegant plaited chain twining around it. In the display cabinet next to it, dazzling, pristine white pillows with the initials of the grand hotel, napkins, starched bed linens. Levadski bows in front of the inconspicuous treasures shown to such advantage by the cabinet lighting. Through the pane of glass he admires a china doll wearing a chambermaid's outfit, holding a tiny feather duster in her hand. The door of the hotel café creaks, perfumed ladies go in and out, their steps swallowed by the carpet, their stilettos taking revenge on the marble in the spacious lobby for the brief hardship endured.

The door creaking behind him, Levadski strides through the soft chandelier light of the café, where the sound of the piano bathes his old carcass. A waiter with a menu in hand emerges from the musical backdrop and shows the guest to one of the tables near the grand piano. Everything is in perfect harmony, the lighting with the carpet, the muted tinkling with the soft glow of the mirror. Only Levadski and the waiter stand out from this somnolent lava for as long as they are in motion. Levadski is already seated. The waiter too, who flits back and forth between the tables, soon becomes part of the furniture. Even in such a small room a person becomes a blur, Levadski is astonished to find, as if the room itself possessed so much soul that we, its true animate souls, suddenly are drowned in it.

The pianist mops his brow and with an encouraging nod and barely audible snort plunges into the keys. *I Did It My Way*. Levadski wants to polish his eyes, which are two dull buttons. The pianist's friendliness is genuine, but it's also pure discrimination. Levadski returns the smile. He deserves it. He who has observed so much. So many waterfowl, nocturnal raptors, diurnal birds of prey, coliiformes, totipalmates and waders, antbirds, the blue cuckooshrike, even calm and sociable Nordic birds such as waxwings, with their beautiful crests. Levadski has observed them, too. He would have given all the fruits of his garden, which he did not own, in exchange for the tinkling warble of the waxwing. Levadski opens the dessert menu. If they eat constantly it is believed there will be a harsh winter. Which is pure nonsense – birds always eat constantly. It is just like breathing. Like thinking.

Semolina dumplings "Old Viennese style" with toasted apricots, 13 euros. The bird eats because this is its way of communicating. Without thought or malice. It talks to the trees through the fruits it eats.

Tarte tatin of apple and pear with walnut brittle ice cream, 14 euros. It talks to the bushes and flowers through the seeds it devours.

Valrhôna chocolate tartlets with cherry sorbet and Mon Chéri, 15 euros. It whirrs along in the perpetual cycle. Harsh winter, either way.

The pianist appears to have found in Levadski an addressee for his noble feelings of pity. In recognition he squints over at him and plays *Bridge Over Troubled Water*.

Iced "Mozart dumplings" with Amaretto foam, 12 euros. The piano player's button eyes flash contentedly during some bars of music, as if there weren't a care in the world. But, my God, it is true: a person who knows music can never be unhappy.

Tiramisu with basil foam and baked raspberries, 14 euros. My mother was in the habit of happily saying. She did not say it to me or to anyone else, but to herself, sighing deeply down at me.

The savory alternative: A selection of local and imported cheeses with nuts and grapes, 15 euros. I too was once no higher than a dining table. What about Beethoven, I could have asked her, how could he be happy as a deaf man?

Levadski orders the chocolate cake. In a matter of minutes it arrives. His memory of it is different. That is, if he remembers it at all. Levadski sinks his fork into the fragile shell of his slice of cake and notices that he feels hot and dizzy. As if a sticky sweet claw were rummaging inside his chest, soft as butter. Suddenly he is a boy, sitting in a church in Lemberg during the midday prayer service. Whimpering, he is sitting on a hard pew, letting the tears roll freely down his stony face. He doesn't dream of wiping them away. He is sitting in the Catholic church like in a jewelry box. He is here to cry in safety until he is exhausted, until he is totally cleansed and free from care. Madly in love, he believes he will die, become crippled and impoverished. Levadski bathes his young face in tears and in self-pity. "Oh Lord, we confess, we are sinners. We are all sinners before you," the priest mumbles. Levadski blows his nose. "And do not turn away from us," the priest prays. Covered in tears, the little martyr looks up towards the ceiling. The Holy Spirit is directly above him, frozen, soaring in perpetuity. Levadski imagines that this dove also has an eye on him, he cannot be lonely, and he cries all the more. "Holy Mary, Mother of God, we pray of you, Holy Mary, we pray of you."

With a sense of elation, Levadski once again turns his attention to his slice of cake. This madness must have gotten into him on that day of the church service. What was the girl's name again? Dunia? Apolonia? Seraphina? Could well be. Not even a name any more. Just these palpitations. What's in a name anyway?

A corpulent gentleman with white combed-back pomaded hair throws his napkin on the table with a dull thud. He wants to pay. He pays and leaves.

"She is in Cyprus playing bridge," an older waiter whispers to a younger waiter in passing.

"Good for her," the young colleague exclaims, without turning around. A tiny piece of silver foil is stuck to his striped trousers. When he turns the corner with a laden tray, the foil is snatched away by a gust of air and washed up beneath one of the tables.

Levadski's eyes wander around the room. The great-aunts sat over there with me, sometimes mother joined us. Over there, where a young couple are toasting each other with champagne glasses filled to the brim. How deeply they look into each other's eyes – disgusting. The world surrounding the two is a gently rippling lake, and they themselves are a boat adorned with flowers. A sinking one. An embarrassing one. A moving one. The only possible and genuine boat at this moment in time. Any second now the young man will notice the waitress's calves and destroy the pastoral.

We sat over there, as well, in one of the window niches. The blue-cushioned seating areas must have only recently sprung out of the walls. There used to be leather armchairs, and the coffeehouses smelled of a world to be taken seriously. Glamorous creatures with feather boas would float past the tables. And I ate my cake and was one of these angels, by virtue of the exquisite breath created by their boas. I was one of them.

"I am accidentally in heaven, I don't eat anything, I don't drink anything ... A little ... I read a good book. I read a good book, and already I am accidentally in heaven ..." The voice belongs to a lady with red painted nails. The lady's hand is vibrating like a bough of a mountain ash as she tells her story. She must be my age. Very elegant, her fringe, that hides the wrinkles of her brow. Very clever. And the black arches of incredulous eyebrows.

"Hair across his eyes, he always wanted his hair across his eyes, but I cut it off during the night." Dark red shred of a mouth. I wonder if she is talking about her son? The way she talks, my God! A stream filled with smoothly sanded pebbles. What a beauty. Levadski orders a tea.

"Green or black?"

"Black, please."

The sight of this gently gesticulating herbarium flower in the circle of her family makes Levadski thirsty. The flower throws back her head and laughs. Crowns of precious metal gleam in her wet mouth. My goodness. What a woman! Levadski drinks and sweats. The son or son-in-law pours the diva some water. Rapt, slightly melancholy faces surround her, while for the hundredth time she tells one of her old stories from times gone by. How she glows! Then she leaves. She is helped into her coat. She throws back her head once more, once more the sight of precious gleaming crowns. Charming soliloquy on the way to the door. The son or son-in-law leads the way, stumbling behind him is the rest of the clan. At the tail end, a child with a short-haired dachshund on a leash.

"Is the lady an actress?"

"No, but she has been coming here every Sunday for thirty years."

"Interesting," Levadski says through his nose. The waiter is already at the other end of the room. "Interesting," Levadski repeats and finds himself boring. Meaningless. For a split second. The waiter is already on his way back. The man whirrs from table to table with the grace of a dragonfly, races, tails flapping, through the rows of tables, almost collides with his two colleagues, walks straight through them.

With withered steps, a couple approaches the table where the beauty was just sitting. The gentleman is wearing a tie and the lady has a brooch pinned to her jacket.

Both are holding a newspaper in their hand. After they have ordered two glasses of sparkling wine, they hide behind their newspapers. The sparkling wine arrives. Cheers! The lady closes one eye when she drinks, as if she had whipped up the sparkling wine to a spray with her breath.

"Here's an interesting article about Transylvania."

"Aha."

"Yes, it interests me."

"Sir and Madam have chosen?"

"Two cream of pumpkin soups, a small veal schnitzel and a small beer."

"I would have preferred duck, but you have run out, haven't you?"

"Do you know why Siebenbürgen is called Siebenbürgen? After the seven cities that the Germans founded in the 12th century."

"Very interesting."

"Excuse me?"

"Very interesting."

"Yes, my darling."

"Yes."

Which direction is she speaking in? Her neatly coifed head slightly cocked like a dove observing its reflection in a puddle, the lady appears to be speaking into a tin can.

"Yes, my darling, yes, alright, my child."

The tin can is snapped shut.

The husband waits for explanations behind the wall of newspaper.

"When our daughters do come, they always arrive late."

The husband turns a page. He must be looking forward to his daughters' arrival.

The main thing is that they are coming. Better late than never. He must be looking forward to it. Nobody is coming to see Levadski. This sad certainty makes him feel superior to the married couple.

"Yes, nuclear power really is a great threat to the world, it will probably be the end of it."

"This is newfangled soup. The pumpkins of our youth, they don't exist anymore."

"Yes, it used be different."

"The pumpkins were never that dark."

Levadski's gaze wanders to an inconsolable face. Two strings of pearls entwine the wrinkly neck they belong to. The old woman turns her head like a blue tit, looks around, before she plucks up the confidence to shakily steer the fork with the piece of cake in the direction of her mouth. She protectively holds her other hand beneath it, chews, swallows, and then, with a critical gaze, chin pressed to her chest, she checks whether any of the cake has fallen onto her lap, her bosom no longer able to catch crumbs.

The red of a broad-shouldered jacket catches Levadski's eye. Barely arrived on the threshold, the female creature with short hair strides towards the nearest waiter. Both come to a stop in front of Levadski's table. "Is there a special Sunday menu today?" the red jacket wants to know. Her earrings are birdcages inset with egg-shaped gemstones. "No," the waiter says regrettably, "the menu is the same as always, but we are serving brunch on the second floor." The lady mumbles something and leaves.

A group of guests traipses through the room. The leader has a sliver of wood in his mouth, which helps to identify him. A lumberjack, springs to Levadski's mind, or perhaps a coffin maker?

A Mr. Sulke arrives and asks for a table for three, father, mother, child. "Sulke is my name," Mr. Sulke says in a deep voice, "we will eat and leave."

"Eat and leave," he repeats. The echo of the name Sulke hangs in the room for a while.

"The worst thing that can happen to you is a stain," the older waiter instructs his younger colleagues, "a stain on a guest is the worst thing that can happen!"

"I mean, I don't begrudge any man for dying his hair, but gray is perfectly fine," a faded beauty assures her friend who isn't exactly a picture of freshness herself anymore. Both of them unleash their venom on a man seated at one of the neighboring tables, whose hair is apparently dyed. His younger companion seems not to be bothered by this at all. She lovingly guides a laden dessert fork towards the open sparrow beak of the man. "Ridiculous," the girlfriends agree. There is nothing cheerful about them, nothing life affirming, thinks Levadski. They won't allow the man anything, neither his dyed hair nor his lover. Under the false pretense of a Sunday breakfast they poison the surroundings with their disgust for life.

Glumly Levadski pours himself tea, and while doing so it occurs to the lid of the teapot to rip away and hurl itself onto the carpet, where it innocently spins around and comes to a standstill in front of the riding boots of one of the girlfriends. She picks it up with two of her varnished nails and brings it over to Levadski, who on his part airs his flat behind and receives the lid with embarrassment.

Shortly afterwards the two leave; the disparate couple also pay and leave. The piano player has left ages ago, something that escaped Levadski's notice, so engrossed was he in his field studies. Levadski has the bill charged to his room. Leaning on his stick, waiting for the golden mirrored elevator, his eyes heavy, watching the coral-colored digits lighting up above the elevator button, 5, 4, 3, 2, 1, M, G, he suddenly realizes that it is he, he is the one who despises life.

M
Zimmer / Room 71–86

IN HIS ROOM, LEVADSKI TAKES A DEEP BREATH. THE AIR IS delicious and sharp, as if a brazen woman is lurking in the cupboard, a smoldering beast with sparkling rings on her cold fingers. Take me out, buy me this and that, protect me, build me a nest! An expectation hovers in the air in Levadski's suite, an invitation, cloaked by an elegantly arranged bouquet of flowers.

Up until now Levadski has not made a present of cut flowers to any living person; he has never had any in his apartment either. Now they close in on him and shamelessly exude their fragrant life in the middle of the table, looming above the exotic fruits, which Levadski wouldn't willingly purchase either, out of protest, and in loyalty to local produce. The flowers are dying, that is perfectly obvious.

Levadski rests his stick against the half open mirrored door to the bedroom and lowers himself into an armchair with a groan. "You too will die," Levadski whispers to the banana in his hand, "not tomorrow, but now. I am going to eat you, not because you taste particularly good to me, but because you are soft, you old banana." As if this weren't enough of a threat, Levadski removes the ball-retained dentures from his mouth. Toothless, he devours the fruit. Bite by bite, if that's how you can describe it. For a split second the gloomy premonition of what perversion is, stirs in Levadski.

When, still chewing, he puts the banana peel back on the plate, something causes his drinking stick to lose its composure. It falls to the floor with a dull cry, but Levadski does not move, does not rush to its aid. "I am too old, child," he says to the drinking stick. Once more, Levadski is overcome by violent palpitations – he has just realized that he is spending more time talking to bananas and walking sticks than he is to people. Not a new revelation, Levadski thinks, getting up and going towards the bed on weak knees, without picking up the stick. He disappears beneath the gold embroidered bedspread in his suit, bow tie and shoes.

It's nothing new, he persuades himself half asleep, to be conversing with your walking stick, it is no big deal, after all, you're all it's got. This isn't merely capricious behavior. You communicated enough with people, even if you were never very talkative. Your posture spoke for you, your gestures and countenance, your behavior, your vivacity. You always reacted appropriately to other people's signals and remained respectfully silent. Was that not communicating? What are you whining about? Levadski snaps at himself. But he is barely listening, the dreamer.

Levadski falls asleep and dreams he is still sitting in the café and waiting for his order. Evening approaches. There are candles burning everywhere. Bored, he watches a couple of lovers kissing and throws up. He tries to throw up as discreetly as possible, into each of the sleeves of his new suit. Without a sound, timorously, considerately, he spews his soul out of his body, until his suit sleeves catch fire. Horrified, Levadski jumps onto the small table in front of him and starts to dance like mad. The lovers are annoyed, voice their outrage and spew the contents of their romantic dinner in the direction of the trouble-maker. The waiter, who has visibly aged, races past the rows of tables with Levadski's order on a silver tray. Too late, Levadski waves him away, the waiter can't believe it. He looks at the floor and then at Levadski, at the floor and then again at Levadski. The lovers grow hoarse from retching, but still they remain in a tight embrace, like two people drowning. Levadski is in flames and dancing, and the waiter, being obstinate, dares to step out onto the ice which a moment ago was still carpet, stumbles and falls and falls and falls …

The memory of the dance in his dream and the fact that he went to bed without getting undressed warm Levadski's heart on waking. He feels like a powerful ruler. Peter the Great is said to have spent the night wearing his riding boots in snow-white featherbeds, which every royal family in Europe considered an honor to furnish him with. This is how Levadski is lying there. Under other circumstances he would not have compared himself to a grand duke, but to a corpse in a coffin. However, in this midnight blue suite, filled with the rotting scent of exquisite flowers, he is what he is not. A booted Infante. It almost gives him physical pleasure to feel shame for his escapades and improprieties.

Levadski sits up in bed. The mirrored door, beneath a battle picture, presents a bald sleepy old man, a hint of despair in his dull eyes, fingers fumbling with the buttons of his waistcoat.

Suddenly Levadski feels a strong desire for a juicy blood-red carnation. Without a carnation in his button-hole he is half a man. "Habib," he pleads in a whiney voice down the receiver, "come."

"Please," he adds, after Habib has already hung up. A few minutes later the butler gently knocks on the door and enters.

"Please be so kind," Levadski asks him from the bed, "and see if you can find a carnation among the bouquet of flowers over there on the table." Habib blinks several times before daring to admit he doesn't know what a carnation is. "A carnation," Levadski laughs, "is a flower. You make a present of it to your teacher after the summer vacation and you scatter it behind a funeral procession."

"Oh, I see!" Habib scratches his neck incredulously.

"And you try not to step on it, just as you try not to step on any other funeral procession flower, otherwise you believe it is your turn to die or that you will lose a close relative."

"A carnation," Habib repeats dreamily.

"Lenin's favorite flower."

"Lenin ..." Habib gushes.

"There must be a carnation among the flowers!" Levadski sighs.

"Was he the first man to fly to the moon?" Habib asks, sniffing the bouquet.

"That was Gagarin, he was first in space." Levadski doesn't feel like laughing. "A carnation, carnation ..." He is dying of thirst. Bleeding to death. "It's probably best if you give me the vase, young man," he says coolly. With one leap Habib is at the bedside. "Damn it! No carnation! Oh well, none then." Levadski shrugs his shoulders and hands the vase back to Habib. "Where were we?" Habib, eyes lowered, remains silent. "Never mind, please help me out of bed. The sun is shining."

"Not anymore," Habib adds, placing the vase of flowers back on the table and helping the capricious hotel guest out of bed.

A little while later and one floor down, Levadski is browsing the hotel restaurant menu, surrounded by the buzzing of two waiters and the humming of nostalgic music. Habib probably thinks I am a lazy and moody capitalist pig. Carnation or no carnation. If he only knew I can't afford this luxury, that I am squandering my fortune because I am ill and that's the only reason I am not counting the cost of the minutes I am staying here, as time is too precious to count. If he only knew that although I keep up my cracked façade, I am essentially on the run from my heart, am in a panic, which incidentally, is alleviated when I look at the appetizers. Levadski inspects the menu through his magnifying glass.

Duet of red king crab with mango and peas in the pod, 25 euros. Levadski imagines the red king crabs singing a duet in a hot frying pan, growing more and more hushed, until only a death rattle is audible, a death rattle that suddenly rises and dies away for a last time. He wipes a tear of laughter from his eye and carries on reading.

Praline of quail with goose liver, young chicory and apple and chervil confit, 24 euros. Confit sounds a bit like conflagration, he informs the waiter, who is busy pouring water into a glass the size of a child's head. With a pained smile he displays his snow-white porcelain ivories to Levadski: Sir, you are pulling my leg. He has never been so serious in his life, confesses Levadski, suppressing a fit of laughter. For a second the waiter's eyes rest on Levadski's magnifying glass. "Give yourself time," he says, rolling his eyes, and flutters from table to table in the direction of the kitchen. Meanwhile Levadski's magnifying glass continues perusing.

Goat's cheese tartlets with smoked catfish and crayfish, 26 euros. A catfish and a crayfish meet. Both dead. Levadski bursts into a fit of laughter. I am ill, thuds in his head, It is a symptom I am forced to tackle like a schoolboy, breaking out into unprovoked fits of laughter, embarrassing myself in front of people, besmirching these magnificent vaulted chambers with my unseemly behavior. An

Who Is Martha?

unmistakable sign of my decay. Giggling, he reads on.

Fillet of Iberico pork with roasted bell peppers and runner bean dumplings, 32 euros. "Cheers," two women at the opposite table toast each other. "To you, my dear," says the woman from the lower pecking order, in a nasal voice. Engrossed in the menu, they compress their pearl-laden concertina necks in an unappetizing way. Both seem familiar to Levadski. Aren't they the friends from the café this morning? How rapidly they've aged.

"Excuse me," he says, detaining the waiter with the porcelain ivories who is sneaking around, "may I ask what the Iberico is?"

"A breed of pig native to Spain and Portugal," the waiter replies, "half-wild, fed on acorns," he adds, topping up his water. "A wild boar!" he whispers into Levadski's wide eyes. Levadski asks for a little more time.

"Such a gorgeous blouse, darling. Well chosen."

"The ladies have decided?"

"We are not talking about you." The waiter disappears. Levadski grins and carries on reading.

Lamb fillet poached in milk of sage and curry, 36 euros. "Have you got horse meat?" Levadski wants to know from the waiter, who has crept up to the table in the hope of finally learning what the guest has decided on. Levadski's question wipes the smile off the waiter's face. The sheen on his pearly whites fades.

"I am afraid not," says the waiter apologetically. "What I can recommend, sir, is a soufflé of turbot on a bed of truffled eggs and green asparagus, very soft and palatable. Or a fillet of veal baked in an herb-pistachio bisque with Pommery mustard puree and Madeira jus. Also very soft." To spite the waiter, Levadski orders the Iberico. The ladies opposite have decided on a four-course menu. "Such a gorgeous blouse, modest, very modest and yet so smart. Not that flowery stuff for housewives and East Bloc grannies that the shops are filled with ..."

"By the way, my nephew," the lady wearing the blouse interjects, "imagine, my nephew recently said to me, 'Granny, you stink.' I cried with laughter, 'Why darling, Granny doesn't stink, that's perfume.' 'Granny, you stink,' just imagine!"

"Enjoy your meal," the waiter arrives, deposits a plate and immediately disappears again.

"The Iberico is going to be a challenge," thinks Levadski, admiring the dramatic composition of slices of meat and circles of smudged sauce through his magnifying glass.

"It's still steaming," the ladies at the opposite table remark, an acknowledgement without envy.

"If only my dentures would live up to the task," Levadski whines, "they are not made for such delicacies."

"What kind of dentures do you have?"

"A discontinued line."

"Porcelain is no good," one of the friends remarks, "it clatters so terribly."

"And often cracks," the other sighs. Levadski nods and turns to his Iberico, pure madness to order, a definite sign of his illness. While chewing, he can sense the concerned glances from the neighboring table.

"Can you manage?" Yes, it's manageable, the pig isn't being too hard on him.

"Soft as butter," Levadski confirms. The ladies express their genuine delight and with a sense of relief continue calmly chatting about all the trivialities that seem to make them happy.

Mollified by the tender Iberico, Levadski grants everyone their happiness. Over coffee his gaze travels from the ladies' table to the bustling waiters, to the intently chewing restaurant guests, to the slender glass vases filled with anthuriums that remind him of polished water lily leaves with a jutting large-pored phallus. Levadski closes one eye.

"A nice man, but the way he treats her, it's atrocious," the friends warble. "Today this, tomorrow that, money for everything, but she had to clean the house herself when she was in an advanced stage of pregnancy ... Perhaps her obsession with shopping ... What could she possibly need, she has money ... Something nice to wear, make-up, the things you need as a young woman ... But in an advanced stage of pregnancy, please. You just want your peace and quiet. Atrocious, I'm telling you, her husband ... The crust is the best ... The salt crust is melting ... On your blouse, darling ..."

Levadski's other eye falls shut. "... Not given to everyone, our luck, a little cream soup," his nose hair antennae inform him, then giving a little grunt, he slumps in on himself like a house of cards. The shifting of chairs revives him again. And again the house of cards falls. Again and again, until the waiter with the porcelain dentures announces into Levadski's left ear that the restaurant is closing.

1
Zimmer / Room 101–128

"You know," Levadski says, placing his hand on Habib's glove, "only yesterday I was shocked to discover that I talk to my walking stick and other inanimate objects more than to animate human beings. During the night I found myself overwhelmed by another observation." Habib peels his eyes wide open. "Yes, yes, during the night I sat up in bed and said to myself: in the few days you have been here in this hotel, you have listened to more people talking and have talked more yourself than you have in the past twenty years. Then I wanted to drink some water, but didn't dare get up. And you know, Habib, nobody was there to help me. I am not saying this as a reproach, I realize you don't work at night, in all my years nobody has ever brought a glass of water to my bedside, I am used to it. And yet, something like pleasure stole over me when I sat there in bed, so helpless. Pleasure at my being among people. Do you understand?" Habib nods, hesitantly withdrawing his hand. "I can now talk to my walking stick with a good conscience, you understand, Habib?"

"You are allowed to do anything," Habib says. There is nothing sarcastic or serious in his voice. Only clarity,

Who Is Martha?

lightness, goodwill.

Levadski imagines the butler's kid glove pressing his hand for a second, amicably, sympathetically, perhaps even with a touch of compassion. That is precisely what he is not allowed to do as a hotel butler and child of the Orient. Who knows how close a young person is allowed to get to an older person in their native land.

"Would you like a sip of water?" Habib enquires.

"It would probably be best if you ran me a bath," Levadski says. Habib moves with measured steps towards the bathroom door, opens it carefully and with a flick of the hand the bathroom is bathed in the light of the chandelier, one of the few gems that Levadski would have liked to have seen in his apartment on Veteran Street.

It would be madness to have such a thing hanging from the low ceiling of my apartment, thinks Levadski as he watches Habib let the water into the bath, it would be madness. Like a widow poor as a church mouse spending her monthly pension on a tin of caviar.

"Bubbles or bath salts?" echoes from the vaulted bathroom.

"Bubbles, please!" Caviar that she would smear on her face like skin cream.

"You know …" Levadski confesses to Habib, who appears in the frame of the bathroom door. "Did you want to ask me something?"

"No, please, go on!"

"But you wanted to ask me something?"

"Yes," a smile plays around one corner of Habib's mouth, "but after you."

"You know, I have a very small apartment. The living room is about the size of this bathroom. And it is full of books. I have to laugh," Levadski smiles, "when I think of my small apartment. What would it say to this chandelier?" Levadski is searching for words.

"It would like it," Habib helps him out.

"You think so?"

"Yes, my family's house would also like the chandelier. But whether they would become a couple, I somehow doubt it."

"Why not?"

"Because we don't have any electricity in our house. Excuse me, the water." Habib goes back to the bathtub. Levadski imagines him taking off his glove and testing the water temperature.

"100 degrees," says Habib in the doorframe, pointing to the blue water thermometer in his hand.

"Correct, always correct," Levadski says in praise and with slight regret. Perhaps genuine closeness does not consist of actual proximity – Levadski allows himself to be grabbed beneath the arms and led to the bathroom – but in the respectful distance which animals are in the habit of affording each other. It is in this distance, and not in an amorphous sticky amalgamation, that human beings are free to think of one another and still be close, to be there for each other, Levadski thinks.

"Careful! Slippery marble," Habib raises Levadski's intertwined arm slightly. After all, thinks Levadski, it is impossible to exist in chaos. You need to rise above it. That's how you maintain perspective. Time is on the side of the observer.

"I have placed a bath towel at the head of the tub," says Habib. That must be the only way you can decide whether you want to be there for someone else, be close to them.

"If you need anything, just call. I am here."

While Levadski unbuttons his flannel pajamas, he can hear Habib fiddling with the CD player in the next room.

"Would you like me to help you get in?" Habib

shouts over the powerful first bars of Beethoven's last symphony.

"No, thank you," Levadski calls out weakly into the swelling emotion of the first movement. He could manage himself, it is only on getting out that he needs assistance. "We have time," he hears Habib.

Square phrasing, pedantic development and shabby creativity is what Stravinsky accused his dead colleague of in this first movement, Levadski recollects. When he dips one foot and then the other into the bubbles, he discovers the long overdue need to cut his toenails. And Rimsky-Korsakov couldn't identify the main connecting thread behind the leonine runs. Obviously he didn't want to, the envious drunkard. Oh no, it was Mussorgsky who was fond of vodka. Where did I read that he always kept a bottle of vodka beneath the table when he was a student at the music academy?

"Tea?" Habib whispers through the crack in the door.

"Thank you," Levadski carefully turns his head in the direction of the door, "would be lovely later."

Oh no, the excessive drinker was Glazunov, not Mussorgsky!

Levadski points his wet forefinger triumphantly at the ceiling.

"Did you call?" Habib rubs his livery against the bathroom door again.

"I was only talking out loud," Levadski says to appease him. Yes, yes, that's the way it was. It was Glazunov who drank the soul out of his body. And it was in a Shostakovich biography that I read about it. Levadski stretches his left leg out of the water and deposits it on the rim of the bath with a dull thud. That's how it was. Shostakovich, as a boy, perhaps thirteen or fourteen years old, arrived at the Conservatory in St. Petersburg, at the time already called Petrograd. During practice the director of the Conservatory, Glazunov, would sit almost motionless at his desk and mumble barely audible words as soon as the recital faded away, more to himself than to his pupils. Glazunov never got up and approached the musicians or their instruments. What chained him to his desk was a rubber hose. It led from his mouth to below the desk where, in one of the drawers, a bottle of hard liquor was stored.

"Habib?"

"Yes, sir?"

"Have you ever heard, oh, do come in, I am covered in bubbles. Have you ever heard the saying, Habib, poor is the pupil who does not surpass his master?"

"The pupil who doesn't pass his master?" asks Habib, hands behind his back, positioning himself next to the bidet.

"Surpass, surpass, be greater than the other."

Habib shrugs his shoulders.

"A baby bird learns more than its parents do," Levadski explains, hiding his leg in the water again. "If the young bird doesn't become a little better, its parents, from a biological perspective, have lived in vain. Laid eggs and died in vain. You understand, Habib?"

Habib shrugs his shoulders again.

"Of course, the child is the death of the parents," Levadski continues, while attempting to unwrap a piece of soap from its gold-green wrapper. "How do you open this?"

"Tear it open in the middle," Habib suggests.

"Yes, death, a death completely in vain, if this baby bird does not surpass its parents by at least half a claw. I would go so far as to claim, poor is the ..." The soap makes a bold leap out of its wrapper into the water. "What did I want to say? Oh yes, I would go as far as to claim that before, before ... I would claim: Poor is the teacher who is not surpassed by his pupil. And foolish is death without fame."

"Well, recognition," Levadski mumbles, "confirmation, if you like." He is annoyed, the words don't sit right, an abyss of countless possible formulations has presented itself just as he wants to complete the sentence.

What is bad, what is bad ..., he continues to formulate in his head, why was it that I called for him anyway, what did I want to say? "Oh!" Levadski gropes around beneath his legs for the soap, "got it! Shostakovich loomed larger for his century than Glazunov. And in spite of this he did not surpass his teacher. You can't compare apples and pears."

"So he never passed him by."

"He did pass him by, but didn't surpass him. Unless Shostakovich drank more than his teacher." Levadski's laughter gives way to coughing. "And then I also wanted to ask you to turn the Beethoven up a bit. Without my dentures I think I don't hear so well."

Habib removes himself on tiptoe. He carefully turns the music up. He has such respect for it, Levadski thinks, for it and perhaps for the miracle of technology, the CD player.

The image of Levadski's first record player, already dated for its time, appears before his eyes. The record player is warming its dust-covered horn in the sunlight entering through the window of the apartment Levadski has just moved into on Veteran Street No. 82. The shelves have just arrived. Three moving men are sitting on the steps of the stairwell and smoking. A neighbor slowly descends the stairs. The moving men take their cigarettes out of their mouths and step aside. A ghost with gray hair piled up high, a gray skirt, gray jacket, mouse-gray socks and dust-powdered shoes with pencil thin heels clatters past them. Her mouth is painted red, the rouge in the crevices of her cheeks reminiscent of the illustrations of mountain ranges in an atlas of the world.

"I bow to you, Madame neighbor!" The young Levadski is standing in the doorframe. His threat of falling to his knees before her is met with a smile and topped off with a nod of the head. "She is accustomed to it," Levadski offers in explanation of his zeal to the moving men, when the neighbor feebly pulls the front door closed several floors down. The movers, who have forgotten to smoke their cigarettes during the laborious descent, throw the burnt-down butts in the tin bucket that Levadski holds out.

"She mutht be over ninety, why doethn't she take the elevator?" the mover with the soft-peaked cap says with a lisp.

"Too proud ..." he says, answering the question himself.

"Don't tell me she knew Catherine the Great!" the lisping man's colleague says, unbuttoning his shirt. A sailboat is stranded in the thick of his chest hair.

"Definitely not Catherine the Great!" Levadski butts in. "If she's really over ninety, then it is possible she was born during the Crimean War of 1853; that she had her first child during the Russo-Turkish war of 1877; her first grandchild would then have been born during the battles of the Russo-Japanese War of 1904, which incurred heavy losses; she will have lost part of her brood in the First World War, and now ..." Levadski raises an eyebrow.

"Go on!" the man with the lisp entreats.

"And now, the long-lived woman, as if things weren't bad enough already," Levadski raises his forefinger, "as if that all wasn't bad enough, the old lady could now throw the rest of her descendants into the jaws of the Great Patriotic War!"

"That'th heartbreaking!" The man with the lisp thoughtfully looks down the concrete steps at the door that the eyewitness to history worthy of adoration has just closed behind her.

"That she has no one, is certain," Levadski assures them. "After all, the apartments in this block are only being given to war veterans."

"That's why the road is called Veteran Street," the sailor with the hairy chest happily remarks.

"Why do you live here? Did you therve at the front?" the man with the lisp wants to know.

"It depends how you look at it. I was ..."

"You've got all your limbs, you're no veteran!" the sailor growls.

"Not an invalid or anything," his colleague with the lisp says, to be more precise.

"I was ...," Levadski fumbles in his pockets, "I was ..."

"You're not a veteran!" The voice of the sailor, too thin for his hairy chest, flapping under the cold vaulted ceiling of the stairwell. "Not a veteran or a fighter, either. Where were you?"

"And where were you, if I may ask?" Levadski says defensively, taking his hands out of his pockets.

"I couldn't." The sailor lights another cigarette.

The lisping man's gaze wanders from the sailor to Levadski and from Levadski to the third mover, who hasn't said a single word so far. "Even our deaf and dumb friend ith lotht for wordth," says the lisping man, tilting his forehead in the direction of the deaf and dumb man who is stretching his tan and oily bald head up high to sniff the words in the air.

"He knowth we are talking about him. We – are – not – talking – about – you!"

"I couldn't," the sailor says, defending himself, "because I, err ..."

"What?"

"Well, why?"

"Because I had to look after my dovecote."

"Errr, hee," the deaf and dumb man howls, pointing with his nose at the matches that are trickling down onto the steps, from the matchbox the man with the lisp is holding.

"I hid in the dovecote, I hid there, there you have it!"

"There you have it, there you have it!" the man with the lisp drones, "the doveth were more preciouth to you than the good old Fatherland! Tho that'th the kind of buddy I have ..." The sailor blinks, as if he had a mayfly in his eye. "Don't tell me that nobody dithcovered you in your hiding plathe!"

"The hiding place was in a cellar," the sailor mimes, buttoning up the shirt he has just unbuttoned.

"Ahha!" the deaf and dumb man gestures dismissively in disgust, "Ahha ..."

"In the thellar," the man with the lisp repeats.

"And where were you, my friend?"

The man with the lisp screws up his lashless eyes before answering. "I have a lithp."

Thunder rolls in the sailor's laugh.

"I have alwayth had a lithp. I wath unfit for the Fatherland."

"Who declared you unfit?" Levadski asks, still standing in the doorframe.

"That'th a thecret," says the man with the lisp.

What kind of thecret, Lewadski nearly lets slip. "What kind of secret?"

"A big one," the man with the lisp jokes.

"Tell us, please!" says the sailor.

"It wath my father. He himthelf wath a chief offither. That'th the reathon."

"Did he die?" The sailor's eyebrows rise. The man with the lisp starts laughing. "Go on, tell us," the sailor pleads.

"I hope tho," says the man with the lisp, wiping one tear of laughter after the other from the corners of his eyes. "I hope tho."

"Ehhe-hee!" the deaf and dumb man says, encouraging him to continue, and rubs himself vigorously on the limestone wall of the stairwell.

"I hope he ith hiding thomewhere in a dovecot and doethn't know the war ith over."

Levadski points his finger at the watch he is not wearing: the shelves still need to be assembled. "The shelves can wait!" the sailor barks, looking at the lisping man with concern, his head looking like a deflated balloon. "If you please," he adds more gently. "We are waiting for your story."

"I am no veteran."

"I thee," the man with the lisp wakes up.

"Ehhe-he!" the deaf and dumb man neighs.

"I was not at the front, but in exile. In Central Asia."

"Wait a minute," the sailor interrupts, "how did you manage to get your hands on a veteran's apartment in this street then?"

"Luck," Levadski smiles, "pure luck."

"That maketh uth even," the man with the lisp says in conclusion, straightening his soft-peaked cap.

"Ehhe-he," the deaf and dumb man adds from the limestone wall.

"He's a clear case," the sailor says and throws his cigarette butt into Levadski's metal bucket. "Unfit because of hearing imp... eh, because he's deaf."

How long ago that was!, Levadski thinks, the bathwater slowly getting cold and the bubbles having disappeared. Nothing is hiding my nakedness. In fact, both of his legs are blowing about like two white flags of surrender at the bottom of the tub. How long ago that was. My beautiful record player, my library yet to be collected. And the neighbor, if she really had been born during the Crimean War, would have been no less than one hundred years old the year that I moved in. It was spring. Or late fall. No, it was spring! Levadski chases away with his arm some remaining wisps of foam. It was March, a time of year filled with hope, when so many women were forced to shed tears, the old ones too. She once came up the stairs with a tear-stained face. With a tear-stained face, and looking disheveled. "Our great leader has died!" she sobbed in the stairwell. If I had not opened my door at the time and seen the old woman's face twisted into a beaming smile, I would have taken her words as a lament from the heart. "Women are crying on the streets and tearing their hair out: what is to become of us, what is to become of us! Thrown to the dogs!"

If I had known it was *he*, thinks Levadski, letting more hot water into the bathtub, the news would have pleased me. That it was *he* who bundled us two and the whole of Chechnya into cattle cars, Levadski raises his scrawny forefinger, that it was for *him* that I bent my back like a mule at the edge of the world – Levadski wriggles into a more comfortable position in the bath – in completely hostile terrain, pure derision! If I had known at the time it was he, I would have embraced the witch in the doorframe and shed tears of joy with her. If she really was a hundred years old, then she was a few years older than I am now.

"Would you like your dentures?" Habib whispers through the slit in the door. In the background the second movement of the Ninth is budding, bees with bodies of metal plate, loaded with pollen of fine iron dust, smashed to pieces on the buds that turn into the flowers of a thorny violin shrub.

"Thank you, I bathe without my dentures."

Habib leaves. Levadski falls asleep. He falls asleep and wakes up as an organ grinder. It is winter. Large snowflakes are hovering around the street lamps and bare branches, a snowflake chases a matron's behind. There is a hum in the air. His hat in front of him on the ground, Levadski starts to grind his organ. A few snowflakes hover around the emptiness in his hat. Levadski carries on grinding – the day has just begun. Soon some change is thrown into his hat. He carries on grinding, gives a nod of thanks for the coins thrown to him by strangers. The lady with the enormous behind is also a welcome sight, her beauty spot compensated for by her head, so like a bird's. A parakeet. How charming, Levadski is pleased, and how practical: arms for grasping, a beak for pecking. A bee-eating couple walks past him, colorful like all coraciiformes. If they were not so lovable I would be compelled to compare them to gypsies, thinks Levadski. The woman promptly turns around and, on the attack, spits a curse at him: Eat and be eaten! Shove off, Levadski says to the wicked woman in his mind. Darling, what's keeping you? her husband, who is standing a little to one side, asks in a guttural display of courtship. Brup-brup-brup, I am coming! the female calls to him. Brhxssrrhhhr! she hurls in the direction of Levadski. No understand, he retorts unmoved. You racist dog! the bee-eater hisses and turns back to her husband. Levadski carries on grinding his organ, he cranks and cranks, and then he sees that his organ is a cat he's pulling by the tail. He carries on cranking, for he wants to earn money, after all. He tries to play *Adieu, mein kleiner Gardeoffizier* on the cat, and immediately the cat turns into his mother's meatgrinder. But Levadski won't be misled. He cranks and cranks. He cranks until the meatgrinder turns into a coffin, beneath the glass lid of which he recognizes his mother's features. And still, he carries on cranking. He plays his song until he collapses.

When Habib helps him out of the cold water, Levadski is ashamed of the joy he feels at the thought of having caught a cold or even pneumonia. It would be simple if he could outsmart the cancer like that. Without any ado, without a battle. Like a lethargic woman, like an Ophelia, Levadski feels like a corpse floating in the water, when Habib, turning a blind eye, holds an outstretched bath towel before him.

"You know, Habib, there is everything in nature, murder, premeditated and otherwise, hunger and plenty, yet more murder of all stripes. The only thing that doesn't exist is prejudice. I have just been thinking," Levadski slips into the bathrobe, "that human thought has produced nothing more unnatural than prejudice." Habib smiles out of the corner of his mouth. "I mean, of what good is it to the human species? Does it get us anywhere? No." Habib nods. "Is there any sense in which it is a precautionary measure for survival? No, for we know the truth in our hearts." Habib nods twice. "Prejudices don't even have an evolutionary selective meaning. So where do they stem from?" Habib shrugs his shoulders. Levadski raps a finger on his skull. "From a sick brain, my friend. What do you think of gypsies?"

"Me?"

"Yes, you, Habib!"

"In a course I attended for hotel personnel on etiquette, how kind of you to mention it, it was recently explained to us that you can't call gypsies 'gypsies' anymore. They are 'travelers.'"

"How silly ..." The bathrobe is too big or Levadski too scrawny. "How heavy the bathrobe is," he says to Habib.

Habib guides Levadski to one of the armchairs.

"Travelers or Sinti and Roma," the butler adds with a concerned expression.

"Not everything at once, at least," Levadski wheezes and takes a seat. "Who came up with the idea?"

"The Minister of Culture?" Habib suggests, liberating himself from Levadski's damp claws. Levadski shakes his head.

"The purists, more likely. It's laughable. When gypsy is actually a beautiful word." Habib agrees with Levadski. You could hear guitar chords and the crackling of a fire at the word "gypsy."

"The gypsies," Levadski turns his gaze away from the mountain melting in the sun, behind which he presumes Habib is standing. "Gypsies are like coraciiformes: powerful torso, short neck, large head, beaks long and pressed flat. I mean the bird." The mountain bows its peak. "I bet," Levadski smiles, glancing over at the bedside table where his dentures have sunk to the bottom of the water glass, "I bet the gypsies, in the course of their cultural history, held in high esteem and imitated the order of coraciiformes, particularly the kingfisher. After all, the coraciiformes and the gypsies are the most colorful birds there are. Seven families: kingfishers, motmots, rollers, bee-eaters, hornbills, hoopoe and todies!" There are three fingers remaining on Levadski's right hand when he counts them up. "Oh!" Levadski exclaims, "I have just thought of a comparison – the seven famous gypsy clans. Hhm. Or was it the twelve tribes of Israel?"

"I don't know, I am from Palestine," Habib admits.

"I don't know my way around history either," Levadski confesses. "One thing is certain, prejudices get in everyone's way." Habib gives a lively nod in agreement with Levadski. Geologically, birds have been around for longer than we have, they are more deserving of paradise than we are! Habib makes a helpless gesture with his hand. "No gray hawk says to a fire-gold three-toed kingfisher: you are too colorful for me. No!"

"No," Habib repeats.

"He just gobbles him up in silence, for it is the hawk's nature. His thought and action are in tune with the laws of the cosmos, my dear Habib."

"He gobbles him up?"

"Of course, and doesn't even say thank you. To whom and for what? Animals don't waste unnecessary words, that's for sure. I, for example ...," Levadski asks Habib to take a seat on the sofa, "I myself am not a bird. I would like to be one, but then I wouldn't be able to appreciate the advantages of my bird existence. I would know how to use it, but not how to contemplate it." Levadski leans over towards the butler sitting stiffly. "I have to admit to you, Habib, deep inside me, when I saw you, I felt a kind of uneasiness, a prejudice against your dark skin." With a light gesture Levadski scatters ash on his head. Habib blinks in hopeful expectation that he will carry on. "You have to understand me, in the region where I'm from, you hardly see people with your skin tone. I was also not used to ..."

"You should see one of the waiters in our restaurant, he's from Ghana. *That's* what I call black. In comparison, I'm pale as a mealworm." Levadski laughs. "We have learned," Habib scratches his chest through his shirt, "that Negros are now called people of color."

"Negro is a beautiful word!" Levadski says outraged.

"You can't say it anymore."

"Nonsense, that would mean the negrofinch would have to be renamed colored finch, those magnificent birds. What happens to the nigrita bicolor and the gray-headed negrofinch?"

"The purists, or whatever they are called," sighs Habib.

Who Is Martha?

"Yes. The purists, those scoundrels, as if there weren't anything better to do. Ask your colleague in the restaurant, or even better, I will ask him myself, what he thinks of the phrase 'people of color.'"

"Better not!" Habib blinks his eyes, "it sounds so offensive."

"Exactly, it sounds offensive."

"I mean the question, it might upset him ..." Habib clenches his lips, leaving only a small line visible.

"Oh!" says Levadski putting a hand to his brow, "that is true. We don't need to ask, do we Habib, since as human beings we already know the answer." Habib nods, relieved. Levadski continues: "Your colleague from the restaurant, did he have color poured on him? No. Is he green, red, yellow or blue? No. He is plain and simply black."

"Yes," Habib nods, "he is black."

"That's why," Levadski folds his hands as if in conclusion, "the word negro, black person if you like, is more apt. I would like to know since when has Latin been abolished? Has it been abolished?"

"Not as far as I know!" Habib shakes his head.

"Perhaps everything is a question of familiarization. Just as I have grown accustomed to your exotic face, I will one day no longer be offended by the word 'colored.' That's fine. It's just the bogus shame and trepidation of the purist crowd that galls me. Do you understand me, Habib?" Habib understands Levadski. He is impatiently sliding around on the sofa. "Perhaps the battle against prejudices is begun on the level of vocabulary and only afterwards on all other fronts?" Levadski looks through Habib and closes one eye. "You probably also have prejudices against us in your homeland, don't you, Habib?" That we are white, gluttons, and above all, that we have good doctors and achieve a ripe old age?" Habib smiles.

"White and gluttonous is just an image, like black and sand-covered. And old age – my grandmother also lived to a ripe old age," Habib grins more broadly, "but only because she didn't have any decent doctors."

2
Zimmer / Room 202–235

STRANGE BOY, NOW HE IS SITTING IN MY SUITE AND IRON-
ing my shirts, polishing my spare pair of shoes ... Levadski
presses the familiar elevator button which instantly turns
into a coral colored square devil's eye. "Greetings from
hell" is what Levadski christens the button. His thoughts
drift to the butler again. Which newspaper would I like to
read, he asked. He would iron it for me, too! The elevator
door opens, a couple, locking hands, staggers past Levadski, exuding a faint smell of fish.

Levadski gets into the elevator, his stomach rumbling.
Today he would manage to make it to the buffet breakfast
in time. He pulls his magnifying glass from his pocket
and looks at his watch. His watch says a quarter to one.
"Oh!" says Levadski, startled. Beside him hovers the hair-
less skull of a gentleman who doesn't appear to be much
younger, but is at least eight inches taller than Levadski.

"Good morning," says the stranger. Levadski returns
the greeting by smiling weakly and pointing at his watch.
"I didn't want to give you a fright," the elegant gentleman
says, passing his stick back and forth between his hands.

"Where are you going?"

"To breakfast."

"Then let's get moving. Just one floor."

"I should really tackle it on foot," says Levadski.

"Witzturn," the stranger introduces himself. Levadski shakes his hand and gives his name. "Go ahead, Mr. Levadski," Mr. Witzturn says when the elevator door opens, "youth first!"

"After you, dear sir." With the silver handle of his stick, Levadski signals at a small party of hotel guests who are waiting in front of the elevator door. But Mr. Witzturn wouldn't dream of conceding.

"I am standing my ground," he says to those waiting. The door slowly closes.

"Excuse me," Mr. Witzturn says, turning to Levadski, who is in a huff, "I feel that I am in the right, as I am the older of the two of us."

"Your feelings deceive you," Levadski mumbles.

"My feelings can't deceive me," Mr. Witzturn growls, wetting his finger and smoothing down his right eyebrow in the mirror.

A pretty boy, thinks Levadski, as smooth as an egg. How old can he be? Eighty, eighty-five at the most!

"That I don't have any wrinkles in my face can be explained by cortisone," Mr. Witzturn explained.

While Levadski tries to remember in what connection he has heard the word cortisone before, the elevator door opens again. "Third floor," Mr. Witzturn says indifferently. "What I actually wanted to do was have breakfast."

"Then let's go!" Levadski tries to hit G with the handle of his stick. After missing several times he finally succeeds.

"Bravo!" Mr. Witzturn says in praise and unsarcastically, and suggests stepping out of the elevator at the same time.

Behind the opening door a tastefully dressed lady with a poodle in her arms stands waiting, its white locks accen-

Who Is Martha?

tuating the pallor of her complexion. If it were black, she would be really elegant, twitches in Levadski's head.

"I will count, one ..." Mr. Witzturn counts, "and then we will step out into the open at the same time, two, three!"

"What a song and dance!" Levadski complains, after the elevator has swallowed the lady with the poodle.

"You are the one who insisted," Mr. Witzturn pants, emphasizing *you.*

"Well, well!" says Levadski, scraping his walking stick on the carpet, "our little trip has evidently made you very tired, you are out of breath." Mr. Witzturn purses his lips.

"I was counting and concentrating, that's all. Somebody had to put an end to this schoolboy prank."

"I am not the one who started it," Levadski said, looking longingly at the door of the café.

"Mr. Levadski!"

"Levadski, if you please."

"Mr. Levadski, I am going through that door now," Mr. Witzturn signals in the direction of the café, "and I am going to devote myself to the reason why I made the effort this morning of shaving and getting dressed, forcing myself into my shoes and taking part in this unnecessary riding up and down. I am going to devote myself to my breakfast. I wish you a good day."

"Be my guest," Levadski's open hand points towards the door.

Mr. Witzturn clatters past the illuminated display cabinets with his stick. "Youth first!" Levadski whispers after him. The narrow back stops as if rooted to the spot and then sets off again a moment later. Levadski waits for the door to stop swinging. Yesterday's waiters dart back and forth behind the milky glass of the café door. In the engraved coat of arms a lion and a stag dig their claws into each other, which stops them from keeling over.

He went left, so I will go right, thinks Levadski, grabbing the door handle. A wall of laughter mounts in front of him, the room to the right is filled with chubby gray-haired women who have strategically sat themselves close to the buffet. "I am sorry," the waiter says regretfully, recognizing Levadski. "Good day, I am sorry, but we have a group of Americans."

"A gripe?" The shrieking wall is collapsing in on the waiter and Levadski.

"No, a tourist party!" It is of no significance, he will find a table, Levadski says cheerily.

"Coffee, like yesterday?" Levadski nods.

"I will bring it to your table!" the waiter promises, and is gone.

The room next door is filled with the sound of Mr. Witzturn's rustling newspaper and the clatter of a female creature's cutlery, who has not made a particularly convincing attempt at piling up her thin hair. "We should consider ourselves lucky for both having that one thing less to worry about," Levadski says to Mr. Witzturn's newspaper.

"Excuse me?" Mr. Witzturn's striking eyes become visible above the newspaper. With the corner of his mouth, Levadski signals in the direction of the strange hairdo of the solitary lady a few tables away. "You are not only a misanthrope but a misogynist as well, Mr. Dawalski."

"My name is Levadski, Mr. Turnwitz. Allow me?" Levadski looks hopefully at the padded chair beside Mr. Witzturn. "Thank you," Levadski says, before Mr. Witzturn can say Please do, and, groaning, takes a seat. Mr. Witzturn lets the business pages drop into his lap, and he gazes disappointed into the distance, into which something valuable seems to be hurrying off.

"You are ..."

"I wanted to apologize ..."

"You are a ..."

"... for my behavior."

Mr. Witzturn allows the words to stand without comment. "I am a lonely old man," Levadski continues, "and seldom among people. My social aptitude has been wirhering away for decades." Mr. Witzturn listens with his head slightly cocked to one side, stroking the handle of the knife lying next to his empty plate. "You haven't eaten anything yet!" Levadski remarks with dismay.

"Yes," replies Mr. Witzturn, "I am scared of the tourist party at the buffet."

"Americans," Levadski shrugs his shoulders, "we can go to the buffet together!"

Mr. Witzturn scans the room. There is not a door in sight, so he concurs.

"I don't understand," Mr. Witzturn admits, "why the fair sex give up their splendid heads of hair with age. They look like men!"

"Who is the misogynist now?" Levadski jokes.

"No, quite honestly, I prefer the lady over there with the ridiculous bird's nest hairdo to those bald chickens."

"Olala!" Levadski says, pleased. "You are getting angry! A blessing, that the ladies are making such a racket. And if any of them had ever made an effort to learn a foreign language like German, the merry club would tear us to pieces like two old traveling clocks!"

Mr. Witzturn closes his eyes, opens his mouth and produces a melodic barking. Levadski also laughs. Armed with his magnifying glass and giggling, he inspects the array of cold and hot dishes at the buffet table.

"Yesterday I came down so late that although the piano was playing, breakfast was over," says Levadski, appraising the shreds of salmon spun with dill cobwebs.

"What did you eat, then?"

"Cake. Chocolate cake."

"Not bad. Right, I am going back to the table now. I find it difficult to stand without my stick." Levadski looks at Mr. Witzturn's ready plate. I am not surprised, that weighs at least a kilo, he wants to say, but pulls himself together and praises the beautiful composition.

"And the small sour pickle on the tip of the tower is the crowning glory! Good luck!"

What shall I eat, thinks Levadski, brutally surrounded by the short-haired women. A boiled egg can turn out to be a cold hard egg, better not go for that. Fruit salad? Kid's stuff. Vitamins have been of no use to me for ages. Venison pâté, liver pâté with green pepper, a moldy French cheese? Horseradish to go with it, a piece of bread that the waiter has hopefully pre-sliced. Yes.

When Levadski arrives at the table, Mr. Witzturn is busy squeezing a wedge of lemon over his salmon. The clattering of the cutlery at the table of the lady with the bird's nest hairdo has become a monotonous stirring in her cup. The waiter has not forgotten Levadski – the coffee he ordered is standing in a silver pot on the table. "What I meant to ask you in the elevator ..."

"A decent portion," Mr. Witzturn interrupts, pointing approvingly at Levadski's plate.

"What I wanted to ask you when you entered the elevator was," Levadski continues, "was, what the time was. My watch stopped."

"It is ten on the dot." Levadski expresses his thanks by smacking his lips loudly.

"That is a very good idea!" remarks Mr. Witzturn on seeing the magnifying glass flashing in Levadski's hand.

"Yes, at least you can see the hands," Levadski jokes. "You learn where the numbers are in the course of life, don't you?"

"You remind me of my first wife," Mr. Witzturn tells

him while pushing a rolled up piece of lettuce into his mouth.

"Did she also have a magnifying glass?"

"No, cancer."

"Oh God," Levadski leans back in his chair, "I am sorry."

"Yes, so am I. It is a menace. The second one also had cancer. I didn't dare take a third."

"How terrible!" Levadski puts the magnifying glass down on the table. "Perhaps that's the reason why I remained a bachelor ..."

"It is never too late," Mr. Witzturn says to a walnut-sized olive eye, before devouring it. "Pitted," he adds after chewing it carefully.

"It is too late for me, Mr. Witzturn."

"Then at least eat."

"I assume," Levadski says over his second pot of coffee, "we were enemies once ..."

"Oh, let's forget the incident!" Mr. Witzturn gestures dismissively with his napkin.

"I am not talking about the incident in the elevator. I mean," Levadski lowers his eyes to the floor, "the war." Mr. Witzturn still insists on forgetting the incident.

"We have," he says, putting the napkin on his lap, "never been enemies."

"It is embarrassing," Levadski crumbles half of Mr. Witzturn's roll, which Mr. Wtizturn follows with a fixed stare, "very embarrassing, that I behaved so impossibly in the elevator. God knows what got into me. If I had known you were a widower, a widower twice over ..." Levadski points a finger at the stucco ceiling.

"Don't you notice anything?" Mr. Witzturn's bleary eyes attempt to hypnotize Levadski. Levadski reaches for his magnifying glass.

"What am I meant to notice? I don't see anything. Oh!"

"What do you see?"

"You have a pimple. Got you, got you!"

"Very funny. Can't you see anything?" Mr. Witzturn's voice assumes an offended tone. Levadski continues to look at him through the magnifying glass.

"You have blue eyes. Green. And one, two, three, four, six little spider veins on both cheeks. Hardly noticeable."

"What else?" Mr. Witzturn demands impatiently.

"You were a good looking man," Levadski says, "and now that you are smiling, I can see that you have dill between your teeth."

"Charming," Mr. Witzturn says in thanks and drinks a sip of tea that he keeps in his mouth discreetly and for longer than necessary. "And now?"

"Already gone."

"You are blind in both eyes, Mr. Levadski, if I may be permitted to make an observation." Levadski puts his magnifying glass in his trouser pocket. "You don't see that I have a plastic nose."

"You amaze me!" Levadski reaches for the magnifying glass again, straining hard to look. "It could be."

"It is! How can you not have noticed it?"

"Well," Levadski says in defense, "I did notice your nose, but I thought, nothing out of the ordinary, the gentleman is partial to the bottle. After all, that is the kind of cultural environment I'm from. You see noses like that sitting on many park benches during summer." Levadski observes Mr. Witzturn's supposedly plastic nose. "And where is the cord?"

"It's a magnetic nose, it is held in place by three magnets," Mr. Witzturn says, crossing his arms in front of his chest.

"Did you lose your nose at the front?"

"Cancer," says Mr. Witzturn dryly and wipes his mouth with his napkin.

Who Is Martha?

"What are your plans for this evening?"

"I don't have any," Mr. Witzturn says, suddenly laughing. "I am laughing because you just wiped your nose!"

"Did I?"

"Yes, with the napkin," Mr. Witzturn reveals, still laughing.

"Yes, I know, I know, it's out of order. Excuse me."

"You only dabbed it a little."

"Nevertheless," retorted Levadski energetically, "it's inappropriate. I am getting old!"

"Never mind, be happy!" Mr. Witzturn laughs raucously, "be happy you can blow your nose as you please …" Levadski grins, Mr. Witzturn clutches his stomach with laughter. "To your heart's desire …" Levadski cautiously laughs along, " … not too briefly and to your heart's desire, oh, I can't take any more, my heart! …" Mr. Witzturn clutches his stomach more tightly. "Get it out, according to all rules of the art! Excuse the expression," a tear-stained Mr. Witzturn adds.

"So what are your plans for this evening? Or are you checking out after breakfast?"

"No, I am staying until tomorrow. This evening I was planning on carousing in the Bar Maria Theresia."

Mr. Witzturn smiles at Levadski. There is still dill between his front teeth, but Levadski decides not to announce this. It will disappear of its own accord while he is drinking tea, he thinks, and smiles at Mr. Witzturn.

"You have got dill between your teeth," Mr. Witzturn says with a concerned face.

"You too," says Levadski peevishly.

"See you this evening, then."

"I will keep you company!"

"Please do. I haven't had such amusing company in a long time. Haven't had the honor of experiencing," Mr. Witzturn says to be more precise and slowly gets up.

3
Zimmer / Room 302–336

"Oh, Habib, you are still here!" Habib is smiling at the pair of shoes he has just worked on with a shoe shine brush. It takes a while for Levadski to follow Habib's gaze. "Thank you! A freshly polished pair of shoes is exactly what I need now. I just met a very pleasant gentleman in the elevator. We are going to meet at the bar this evening."

"But at the bar, people won't be able to see your shoes that well. It would be different at a concert. At a concert you parade up and down during intermission in the gala lights!" Habib swings his arms as if he were marching. "And everyone sees: your shoes are polished."

"Is there a concert in the hotel?"

"No, but right behind the hotel, in the *Musikverein*."

"Oh! Goodness ..." Levadski feels an icy caterpillar placing a series of sharply polished eggs in one of his ventricles. "The *Musikverein* ..."

"Is right behind the hotel."

"I know, I know, I had just forgotten ..."

Levadski crosses the room and stops in front of the window.

"On the other side, this is the Ringstrasse boulevard,"

Habib explains.

"Yes, of course, behind the hotel. I have been there."

"You have been there?"

"Yes, it was a very long time ago." Levadski has to take a seat. He hands his stick to Habib. "The *Musikverein* ..."

"A concert every day."

"This evening too?"

"Yes, several. One in the Glass Hall, one in the Stone Hall, one in the Metal Hall, one in the Golden ..."

"Golden Hall," Levadski sighs, "golden sound!"

"If you would like tickets, I am happy to arrange some for you," Habib says, holding Levadski's stick in his hand. "The *Musikverein* is a must, especially when you are staying in such style as you are."

The butler assumes the proportions of a mountain in front of Levadski, who is dozing off in his armchair. "A long time ago with my great-aunts," Levadski sighs, "I had a long pair of trousers sewn especially for the *Musikverein* ..." Levadski's eyelids, paper-thin in the sunshine, quiver with every movement Habib makes. Or is it the branches of the trees that are swaying in the wind in front of the window? It grows even lighter behind Levadski's lids. "And the little titmouse," mumbles Levadski, "can you hear it calling! Zib-zib-zib, beyond words the way it intones. It sounds midnight ..."

Levadski's chin slides feebly onto his chest, his right ear tilting towards his shoulder, as if his left ear wanted to listen to what was happening on the top floor of the hotel. Levadski's suspicion is confirmed in his dream. He takes his socks off and sees for himself that his feet, which feel unusually hard, are really hooves. Habib is murmuring some kind of incantation over his shoulder. Tramp tramp trampaloo, here's a flower just for you. White, yellow, inky red, for tomorrow you'll be dead!"

"Stop it!" Levadski interjects, "it's not funny." Habib apologizes, he only meant to help. Hips swaying, he prances toward the door and leaves the room.

"Tramp, tramp, trampaloo …" Levadski hears Habib singing in the corridor.

I can't chop off the hoof, Levadski concludes, I can only affirm my cosmetic defect. And I can wash it. Levadski stomps into the bathroom and dips his hoof into the full bath. Thick steam rises towards the gilded domed ceiling.

"Hell, hell, hell!" Habib is singing in the bedroom.

"Why has he come back?" The steam is growing thicker and thicker, the water is spouting green bubbles that glisten for an excruciating moment before they burst. But Levadski does not allow himself to be led astray. He sits clinging to the side of the bath, letting his hoof dangle in the soup.

"Hell, hell!" Habib sings. The bursting of the bubbles grows louder and louder. It swells to the sound of thundering cannons.

"Damn, it's wartime!" Levadski tries to pull his hoof out of the bath.

"For the Fatherland! For the Fatherland, from the mountain and from the valley, up and onward, fresh and cheery!" utters Habib from the bedroom.

Levadski is shivering with exhaustion. He cannot lift his legs any more. In a green bubble he suddenly recognizes the meticulously shaven face of his new acquaintance from the elevator. "Mr. Witzturn! It's wartime!" Levadski moans.

"Come, brother, give me your hand!" he hears Mr. Witzturn say in a mosquito voice from inside the bubble.

"For the Fatherland! For the Fatherland!" Habib yodels through the bathroom door, "the land where our cradles stood …"

Who Is Martha?

Levadski stretches his finger out towards the greenish bubble. "And what if you burst?"

"Don't worry, soon the days of ice and powdery snow will be over. Please!" Mr. Witzturn pleads from his filigreed hiding place. Levadski hesitates. The blister of water is trembling precariously. "Quick, brother, give me your hand!" Levadski moves his finger in the direction of Mr. Witzturn's plastic nose, coming closer and closer. "For the Fatherland, for the Fatherland!" Habib shouts in Levadski's ear. The finger twitches and bursts the bubble.

"Mr. Levadski!" Habib's kid glove holds on tightly to Levadski's wrist while Levadski is racked by a coughing fit. "You were snoring," Habib tells him between coughs, "and then you choked in your sleep. Do you want me to thump you?" Levadski shakes his head.

"Do you think you could, ahem, get me two tickets for this evening?"

"But of course. A lady?" Habib rolls his eyes gallantly.

"Ahem," Levadski clear's his throat, "the gentleman from the elevator. I have always, been, ahem, suspicious of women, people too by the way. Humans on the whole, I mean."

"I understand." Veils of clouds drift across Habib's moon-face. "Don't get me wrong, he-hemm. Habib, I am not a ladies' man, and where I worked, I only drank with colleagues, he-hem-aheeheem, because I was forced to."

"I understand," Habib repeats even more softly.

"And now I am here, Habib, the *Musikverein* is behind me. On one of the upper floors, my acquaintance from the elevator, a particularly amiable gentleman, is enjoying a nap, isn't he? Tomorrow he is leaving. I will never see him again. Why, for God's sake, should I not invite him to a concert and give him some pleasure?"

"I will arrange the tickets for you."

"Music," Levadski adds, eyes screwed up in delight, "wipes away all misunderstandings. It sweeps across the world!" Habib takes a peek at his watch. "It sweeps across the world as the only, the only truth, Habib!"

"Yes," The butler sighs.

"I do not know the gentleman. But that is beside the point. We are," Levadski searches for the words, "we are symbols."

"Of what?"

"Well, symbols of, ahem, of those, of those ..." Levadski scratches his bald head, "of who we might have been. Of who we are!"

"Let's hope that your friend can make it," Habib remarks carefully.

"Why shouldn't he be able to? After all we have arranged to meet in the Bar Maria Theresia this evening." Levadski throws a glance at the telephone. "Would you be so kind as to find out which room Mr. Witzturn is staying in?"

Habib calls the concierge. "The name is Witzturn. Witz ..."

"Turn!" Levadski adds.

"Turn, Witzturn, yes. Yes. Thank you. We're joining forces." Levadski struggles out of the armchair.

"Oh, Habib, please ask him whether he would like ..."

"Yes. Good day, reception. I apologize for disturbing you around ..." Habib looks at his watch, "lunchtime. The gentleman you arranged to meet this evening in the Bar Maria Theresia would like to know whether you would care to go to a concert with him instead. Yes. Yes. Classical music. Yes. Vienna Symphony. We will let you know in a minute what time it starts. Thank you. Yes, thank you. Yes, I will pass that on. Thank you. I will. I will. Goodbye."

Habib raises his forefinger. "He would be delighted to

join you, but he wanted me to tell you that the concert does not get you out of paying a visit to the bar!"

"Did he really say he would be delighted?"

"Yes, absolutely delighted!"

Levadski taps his scrawny thigh. "That's the kind of man I met in the elevator!"

"Here, the program," Habib waves a magazine. "Where To Go In Vienna, *Musikverein*, November. Today … Wednesday, November 10, 2010, 7:30, Fe-do-se-yev. Vladimir Fedoseyev, conductor, Alexander Glazunov, there he is, your Glazunov, Concert Waltz No.1 in D-Major, Op. 47 and Concerto for alto saxophone and strings in E-Flat Major, Op. 109, and after the intermission, Hector Berlioz, *Symphonie Fantastique*, Op. 14, Episode in the Life of an Artist …"

"That sounds good!" Levadski says happily, "please call!"

"Yes. Good day, reception again. It starts at 7:30. Vladimir Fedoseyev, Conductor, Alexander Glazunov, Concert Waltz and Concerto for saxophone and strings, Hector Berlioz, *Symphonie Fantastique*, Episode in the Life of an Artist. You could think about setting out slowly at 7:00. The *Musikverein* building … Yes, seven o'clock, it's right behind the hotel. You know. Certainly. Seven in the lobby," Habib repeats and nods at Levadski on the opposite side of the room. "Enjoy yourself. Goodbye."

"Why did you say reception? You called from my room."

"Your friend, Mr. Witzturn, he does not have butler service."

After several failed attempts, Levadski hoists himself out of the armchair. Smiling and serious, he is now standing before Habib, who makes himself smaller by lowering his gaze to the parquet floor. "You are a wonderful person, Habib." If the butler were to raise his gaze from the parquet floor now, he would be looking into Levadski's watery eyes.

"Have a rest before the concert," Habib advises and takes his leave so that he can arrange the tickets.

Such a tactful young man! Levadski looks at himself in the mirrored door of his bedroom. The suit was a good buy. And the walking stick too. I will take a discreet look at Mr. Witzturn's cane through my magnifying glass this evening when the opportunity arises. Levadski trots over to the window: a streetcar, red, light gray and gray, swims along the tracks.

Want a real vacation? the advertisement on the first car reads. *Tunisia, only two hours by plane. Live your dreams!*

When Mr. Witzturn is clapping this evening, I will seize the moment and take a look at his walking stick, thinks Levadski.

I am moving ahead, reads the ad on an older red streetcar on the other side of the road, *Vienna-businesschool.at*.

It is impossible for a human being to have as much tact as this Habib, thinks Levadski. Like an animal, yes, like an animal he holds up a mirror in front of me, the mirror of my own wretchedness.

Toifl Textile Care is waiting in the middle of the street, blinkers on, and turns off in the direction of the back entrance of the hotel. *15 Years Gruenfeldt Insect Screens* breathes in the exhaust from the little Nordsee fish delivery van. *Fall in love with fish*.

If I were Habib, it would never have occurred to me to announce myself as the reception desk, such thoughtfulness, so tactful, such genuine sympathy! Just so that Mr. Witzturn is not reminded that there are people who are even more privileged that he is in this hotel. Or perhaps so as not to make me seem like a show-off? Levadski stares at the writing on the streetcar that slowly comes to a halt in front of his window. *Nobody chooses where they are born.* Mr. Witzturn probably has sufficient dignity to not feel one iota smaller in a Classic Room and without a butler. But you never know. At our age.

The ringing of the telephone gives him a start. Habib is on the line, he has got the tickets. Row 1, seats 3 and 4, ground floor box on the right, sparkling wine in the intermission ordered in Levadski's name.

You are a treasure, Habib, Levadski wants to say. "You have done me a tremendous favor," he slurs into the receiver and hangs up. My goodness, hard to believe. *Musikverein.* Great-aunts! Suddenly he feels a shiver run down his crooked spine. His great-aunts, what if they are still alive! He never received any death notices. Oh come on, Levadski thinks, they passed away long ago. Both of them. Their graves must have been leveled at least fifty years ago to make room for new great-aunts. Nobody who has ever made inquiries about reserving a plot in a cemetery believes in the fairy tale of eternal peace. All a sham. I won't be bumping into them in the *Musikverein*, thinks Levadski, unsure of whether to be sad or relieved, but I will raise a glass of sparkling wine to the darling dead. And to mother, who never managed even once to come along, as she was always working. The poor thing. I will drink to mother later, at the bar.

Flight PS 819
Non-Stop
Flight time 2 hours

AT 7 P.M. ON THE DOT LEVADSKI SEES THE GLEAM OF MR. Witzturn's silver cane handle on the stairs. His steps are muffled on the red runner and echo on the marble of the lobby. Leather shoes, thinks Levadski, extending his hand to Mr. Witzturn. "I thought," he joked, "that we would bump into each other in the elevator again." Mr. Witzturn pants and laughs, he had wanted to get a bit of exercise and decided to take the stairs at ten to seven in order to arrive in the lobby on time.

"Five floors," he says, fluttering his eyelashless lids as if he himself refused to believe he had just managed to master them. Levadski doesn't believe it either. I bet he got out on the second floor and then took the steps, the old windbag.

"Impressive, impressive," Levadski praises Mr. Witzturn. "So your room is on the top floor." Mr. Witzturn nods and whispers meaningfully:

"Above the tops of the trees!"

"Let's go," Levadski suggests, waving two tickets printed on shiny black paper. Only after Levadski has politely nodded at a doorman with gray hair at the temples does Levadski realize that Mr. Witzturn has followed him through the revolving door, rather than him going first. "For heaven's sake, Mr. Witzturn, please forgive me!" Mr. Witzturn's mouth is twisted, he is trying to suppress a laugh. "One doesn't get any younger," he says coughing. "As an old man I am used to the youngsters being in the fast lane."

A flock of perfumed matrons with fat ankles noisily totter past the two of them. "In the old days," Mr. Witzturn recollects enthusiastically, "if you were a lady, you had a feather boa and moved as proudly and silently as a marble column."

"Hhm, hhm," says Levadski in a huff.

"One let oneself be worshipped like an icy mountain peak," Mr. Witzturn says, waving his hand in its leather glove. Levadski grumbles and looks into the illuminated window of the restaurant, where yesterday he nearly dislocated his jaw on the Iberico. "For the conqueror," Mr. Witzturn skips on, "the air grew thin around them, and some lost their lives in the ascent, isn't that so?"

"You probably know better, I have never been a ladies' man," Levadski shrugs his shoulders.

"And those long languishing lashes, double rows of pearls, those scamps!" Mr. Witzturn says intoxicated, his voice sounding increasingly tender, as if a sharp-edged sliver of candy were melting beneath his tongue. "And now this," he says dryly, signaling with his head in the direction of the matrons in their clodhoppers hurrying away.

"Do you like classical music?" Levadski asks while crossing the street.

"Oh!" Mr. Witzturn exclaims, "I wanted to thank you so much for taking me with you today. I love music."

"Wonderful," Levadski says pleased, "I also love music, and Glazunov is one of the greats. A drinker!" he murmurs, causing the two women wearing trousers in front of them to turn around in alarm. "A drinker and a genius!" Levadski adds decisively, "one of the Russian greats!"

"Those two gentleman are showing us the way," Mr. Levadski says to the backs of the trouser wearers, "the entrance must be there."

"Have you ever been in the *Musikverein* before?" Levadski asks, keeping an eye on the steps, which he takes elegantly, according to his strength, one after the other.

"Yes, a hundred years ago," Mr. Witzturn laughs, overtaking Levadski. "This evening, with your permission, I will lead the way."

"That suits me fine. You are also the taller of the two of us," Levadski cheerfully hurls at his back. "I almost feel like a female blackbird during the breeding season beside you!" he admits, breathing laboriously in the lobby.

The few steps have also taken their toll on Mr. Witzturn. "I like you," he splutters, leaning against a column, "I like you, Mr. Levadski, although you have a lousy character." Levadski expresses his horror by letting out a low whistle. "But I presume," Mr. Witzturn adds, "that the lousiness of your character has gotten worse with age."

"What a consolation," Levadski says by way of thanks, looking around.

In the meantime the clodhoppers have dropped off their coats and are assessing – so it seems to Levadski – each other's miserable festive attire. "Very shabby." Mr. Witzturn confirms, following Levadski's gaze.

"Oh, I have forgotten my magnifying glass!" Levadski says, slapping his brow.

"And the tickets?"

"Those I have, although nobody has asked to see them."

"We are not in the auditorium yet," Mr. Witzturn says

to placate him.

"We will not be sitting in the auditorium, but in a ground floor box. First row."

Mr. Witzturn clamps his walking stick between his thin legs and takes off his coat. Levadski skilfully receives it and is rewarded with a beaming smile from Mr. Witzturn. "Stay here, I will drop off our coats."

"Allow me the honor, Mr. Levadski." When Mr. Witzturn has returned, Levadski hands him the program he has just bought. "I am really looking forward to this."

"Let's go," says Levadski, "I will smooth the way through the crowd."

"Strange, they didn't check our tickets at all," Mr. Witzturn remarks, making himself comfortable in an upholstered chair.

"They did, you just didn't notice. There was a young lady at the entrance to the box."

"Oh, I see, that's reassuring."

"Why reassuring, if I may ask?"

"That we are not taking the state for a ride," Mr. Witzturn laughs into the audience. "Look, look, one gray wave after the other."

"What do you mean?"

"I mean all the old fogies in a festive mood," whispers Mr. Witzturn, stroking his bald head.

"If you screw your eyes up slightly," Levadski whispers derisively, "all these people look like the sea on a cloudy day."

"And those people over there!" Mr. Witzturn tries to keep his forefinger in check, "that woman looks like a lampshade."

"Perhaps because she is wearing a hat?" Levadski suggests.

"True. But my God, how tasteless. I mean, if you are

that ugly you should at least try to put yourself in a good light by wearing unobtrusive jewelry and modest attire."

"By having winning traits, a friendly smile, a warm heart," Levadski goes on listing.

"Unfortunately I can't see the lampshade."

"Oh!" Mr. Witzturn exclaims, "one second!"

"Where are you going?"

"One second."

"They are about to begin."

"Yes, I will be back."

"You will trip in the dark. Where are you going?"

"To wash my hands!" Mr. Witzturn mumbles, forcing his way past Levadski.

He really could have thought about that earlier, thinks Levadski and gazes at the surging sea in front of him. Here and there he registers a bright red dress, a light blue scarf, a made up black-haired beauty, jammed between two rotten mushrooms. His heart pounding, he registers the golden tone of the brass instruments on the stage, white nymphs, golden nymphs with shapely arms, the wood of the coffered ceiling. Where has the old boy gotten to? Levadski is beginning to feel uneasy. In the auditorium and in the balconies people are taking their seats, the lights of the large pear-shaped chandeliers are being dimmed. Slowly the chandeliers rotate as if they were being roasted on a spit, heated by people's breath, and if everyone were suddenly to grow silent and freeze, Levadski swore, you would be able to hear a gentle tinkling from the casing of the chandeliers.

"Voilà!" Mr. Witzturn pants in Levadski's ear, "a present for you," proferring a little black velvet case that feels quite heavy in Levadski's hand.

"What is it?" Levadski whispers.

"Open it."

"What's inside?"

"Open it and take a look yourself. I chose it from the selection in the glass cabinet of the hotel," Mr. Witzturn lets slip, before Levadski opens the small black box.

"You have gone mad."

"Open it, open it!"

"You are crazy."

"Come on, open it."

"Don't tell me you just went back to the hotel."

"No, I didn't," Mr. Witzturn giggles.

"Gentlemen, a little quieter if you please!" a male voice barks out of the dark.

"I bought it for you this afternoon," Mr. Witzturn tries to whisper more softly, "and I forgot the package in my coat pocket. Come on, open it."

"You are embarrassing me," Levadski whispers and opens the black box without making a sound. "Opera glasses!"

"As I know your penchant for magnifying glasses ..."

"Oh, and how beautiful they are! With a gold chain!"

"It says Luxury Collection." Mr. Witzturn points to the gold lettering on the inside of the box. "I thought they would suit you."

"Be quiet!" a female voice entreats, before succumbing to a severe prolonged coughing fit.

"We can only reciprocate the entreaty," Levadski whispers to Mr. Witzturn, in the hope that the message reaches its true destination. He takes the binoculars from the box and puts the long chain around his neck. With an enchanted smile, Levadski looks through the opera glasses onto the stage and sees – nothing. He sees a lot further, into his own pleasure. Mr. Witzturn's presence fills Levadski with a kind of intoxication, a growing feeling of triumph that conquers everything in its path. He could fell trees, he could perform a saber dance, yes, he would defeat a saber-toothed tiger in battle, all because he had been given a present with a single thought. "I don't know how to thank you," Levadski murmurs.

"You're welcome." Mr. Witzturn has raised his head, his gaze rides on the waves of gray and dyed hair, stumbles over a few bald heads and is lost in the froth of the music. He closes his eyes. Levadski tries to concentrate on the music, but he can't. The elegant opera glasses around his neck have conjured up a new being from inside him and sat him on his lap. They suit me, he said, thinks Levadski and looks at Mr. Witzturn, who, with his eyes closed, has started swaying on his chair. Luxury Collection ... Mr. Witzturn gives a soft grunt and touches his chest. And again he gives himself up to the music.

During the intermission a silver tray with two glasses of sparkling wine filled to the brim sit on a bistro table, a folding card with the name Levadski placed in front. "You are famous," Mr. Witzturn jokes, grabbing a champagne glass that splashes as he holds it out to Levadski. He pulls the other towards him a little more carefully. "I love music, and I would like to thank you for the enjoyable entertainment this evening," Mr. Witzturn says, taking a sip from his glass. "Your visual aid really suits you." Levadski strokes the opera glasses resting on his belly.

"You have moved me to tears, Mr. Witzturn."

"Wait a second. I will read something to you. Please hand me the box." Mr. Witzturn unfolds the leaflet with the instructions. "*Room with a view.* That must be what the thing is called. *Cast your eye down on the angels!*" he recites in a distorted voice. "*For more than 135 years they have been looking over the shoulders of the great maestros on the podium of the Vienna Philharmonic,* well, one doesn't live that long ... *With an eye for detail,*" Mr. Witzturn continues with a raised finger, "*focus on the essence. These*

Who Is Martha?

elegant opera glasses open up undreamed of perspectives, oho-ho, *and unknown pleasures,* enjoy, Mr. Levadski. Enjoy the world of music. And thank you for the sparkling wine." The tears in Levadski's eyes cause his already distorted vision to become even more blurry.

"Oh, you have given me such a wonderful present. You know," Levadski dries his tears under the false pretense of gazing at the ceiling submerged in thought, "I must confess something to you." Mr. Witzturn nods. "I have always been a bit ashamed of my magnifying glass. And now that I am holding these beautiful opera glasses in my hand," Levadski's voice trembles, "ehehem, the good old magnifying glass is just embarrassing, so embarrassing, that I would like to bury it somewhere." Mr. Witzturn tilts his head and chews on his lip. "What can I say ... I know every scratch," Levadski continues, "even the circumstances under which the magnifying glass received them ... and now, alongside these beautiful opera glasses ..."

"You don't need to feel bad," Mr. Witzturn interrupts, "life is unfair."

"I do!" Levadski says heatedly. "But just how fair life is!"

"Please allow me to explain to you," Mr. Witzturn says, putting his empty glass decisively on the table.

What a conceited oaf, thinks Levadski, and I thought he was congenial! I will hang his opera glasses on the wall and let them gather dust there.

"You see," Mr. Witzturn says, "we are in the well-heated *Musikverein*, drinking sparkling wine and being transported by music." You were reveling in sleep, you snooze bucket! thinks Levadski.

"But that does not in the least," Mr. Witzturn continues, "mean that luck is on our side. If the world we know, the visible and the invisible, is a kind of river, then we aren't sitting in a concert at all." Mr. Witzturn looks at

Levadski expectantly.

"We are in the intermission of the concert and we are leaning on a bistro table."

"We cannot be sitting here in the ground floor box for the more privileged, Mr. Levadski, because, and now I need to take a deep breath, because everything is flowing. Everything is changing." Levadski's eyebrow, in the guise of a thin caterpillar, creeps up towards the plateau of his head, oblivious to the fact that nothing is growing there. "While we sit here in the warm hall, having a civilized conversation, smartly dressed, we are both lying in the gutter half frozen to death with liver disease ..."

"Haha!"

"... an ignoramus bringing a child into the world to a working class family ..."

"Hahaha!"

"... sweating in a deep coal mine in India, hooligans urinating from a bridge in London ..."

"Ha!"

" ... and are thrown behind bars for the tenth time ..."

"Muhaha!"

" ... while we were whizzing up and down in the elevator of our hotel ..."

"I thought you took the hotel stairs, you athlete!" Levadski clutches his stomach with laughter.

"... while we were pressing on the buttons in the elevator and consuming electricity," Mr. Witzturn continues, eyes firmly shut, as if he were standing in the pouring rain, "while we were helping ourselves to chocolates from the cake rack and drinking coffee from cups that were far too small, dressed up like two peacocks ..." Mr. Witzturn smacks his mouth bitterly, "I don't know where you were, Mr. Levadski, but I lay between the corpses of my comrades in my own excrement, shooting at people I didn't know."

"Please take your seats!" a young man shouts into the crowd of buffet guests.

"This doesn't mean I am so moved by this knowledge that I cannot either appreciate or enjoy life, Mr. Levadski." Mr. Witzturn hastily adds, releasing his finger from the tabletop. "Now, more than ever, I am pleased about the illusions I see. Do you know the magic lantern?" Levadski nods and follows Mr. Witzturn to the box. "I presume we live in such a thing. All of us. All human beings."

"But not the animals!" Levadski places his hand on his heart. "Not the animals!"

"As far as animals are concerned, I don't have a clue," Mr. Witzturn says, grasping the door handle to the box. "All I wanted to clarify with my monologue, which is evidently a source of amusement to you, is that we human beings, when we speak of fairness, are talking about a chimera. There is no fairness. There is only fortune and misfortune, two sides of one coin, and something better still."

"And that would be?"

Mr. Witzturn lets Levadski pass, closes the door to the box behind him, leans his walking stick against the wall and says:

"Pleasure in pleasure."

Impressive, thinks Levadski in the dimming lights of the ground floor box, and ripe for the stage. Human beings have already come a long way with this all-relativizing belief in a kind of multiple dimensionality of the world. And have always just run around in circles. Loud noises, dramatic curves of tension, a confusion of speculations and exhaustive explanations. But in the animal kingdom, Levadski squints over at Mr. Witzturn, who has closed his eyes again, in the animal kingdom there is no room for this kind of maybe here, maybe there, magic lantern show. There an aged blackbird sits on the tip of a birch tree and chirps the soul out of its body like a young thing, without respite, unshakeable in its love of nature, for the other blackbirds, for its own little life, and the next moment, on account of its age, breathes its last in mid-song. That is true fortune.

Annoyed, Levadski has to admit to himself that once again he is not capable of concentrating on the music. He is not even interested in the faces of the female musicians. This would be the ideal time to make use of his opera glasses. But no, Levadski is sulking in the darkness of the box beside the chirping Mr. Witzturn. The more he chirps, the more he moans in his sleep and twitches his legs, the more Levadski hates him. He must be on the chase, the old hand, Levadski thinks, a bat out of hell. Or did he mean to clarify with his trench story that he has lived a more intensive life than I have? Clever, very clever. And how narcissistic, at the expense of all those dead ...

Meanwhile the first movement of the symphony, along with its dreams and passions, is drawing to a close. The unhappy lover tastes the all-consuming fire of love and settles himself in the shade of a tree to contemplate his precarious situation. The *Symphonie Fantastique* was never my thing, Levadski thinks, so it doesn't matter much that the expensive tickets were a waste – one of us is sleeping, the other is annoyed. And Berlioz himself is also an ambivalent figure in the history of music, it's very brave of the director of the *Musikverein* to include this musical adventurer in the program, and Glazunov as well, who was essentially a talentless, whiny boozer. Courageous of the conductor and the orchestra, they're playing the two of them for all the pseudo friends of music like myself in such a moving way, in an attempt to bring us to life. To hell with music!

With a clumsy gesture of his arm Levadski gives the

armchair a thump, along the upholstered back of which Mr. Witzturn's body flows like dough being forced into a suit and shoes. At least he should pull himself together. After all, the tickets weren't free. As far as I am concerned, I am a lost cause for the rest of the evening. Levadski shakes the sleeve of Mr. Witzturn's jacket.

"What do you want?"

"Oh, excuse me, I thought ..."

"That I had fallen asleep?" Mr. Witzturn asks sleepily. "It is my right, as a visitor to this noble establishment, it is my primary duty," he prattles, "to give myself to the music as I please. So, please." While Mr. Witzturn's eyes close again, forming two velvet pits, his prominent lower lip swells to an obscenity.

Old crank, Levadski curses in his mind, that's how he dares to snub me.

The second movement erupts boisterously and a little capriciously over Levadski. A ball, a ball! The love-crazed artist is dancing his feet off beside the creature he worships. A chimera leads the infatuated lover by the nose. He allows himself to be led and misled, thinks Levadski, whereas in the animal kingdom nature won't tolerate a display of courtship for longer than necessary. But the second movement doesn't last very long either. A ball, intoxication, a pile of broken glass.

What filthy instrumentation, the repellent harmonics almost make me want to wash myself! Levadski pulls a handkerchief from his trouser pocket and mops the three furrows of his brow. He dries his turkey neck, his eyes; filled with disgust, he wipes his mouth. In the darkness the handkerchief looks to him like it is smeared in blood. With a cry of dismay Levadski throws it on the floor.

"Quiet!" a woman's voice hisses from the auditorium. Mr. Witzturn doesn't stir. Levadski carefully feels his face, looking for a wound, but he can't find anything. He gropes around between the legs of the chair for the handkerchief, gets a hold of it and resumes an upright position wheezing, the handkerchief trapped between two fingers. He hits his head hard on the balustrade, and while the handkerchief flutters to the floor again, Levadski, albeit briefly, without inhibition announces his pain to the Golden Hall of the *Musikverein*.

Mr. Witzturn is startled out of his dream. His scream, occurring only a split second later, joins Levadski's wail of pain, expressing itself as a distorted echo.

"What a scandal, the two young rascals in the box!"

Levadski can feel the eyes of the concertgoers glaring with anger in the darkness of the auditorium.

"What did you shout at the people?" Mr. Witzturn whispers.

"Nothing," Levadski whispers back, "I just banged my head in a very unfortunate way and let off a sound."

"Hhm. If it was a noise from your mouth, I can't see anything criminal in that. Unless of course ..."

"If you are trying to say I fa..."

"That would be forgivable too."

"If what you are trying to tell me is that I, during a concert, would, well ..."

"Throw them out!" says the infuriated female with the smoky voice, which could easily have been mistaken for a pubescent boy's. Mr. Witzturn sits up in his armchair and with an absentminded gaze concentrates on the third movement, which has just opened to the sound of two oboe instruments conducting a romantic *parlando*. Right into the thick of it, the genius in love staggers, sad, lonely, forsaken by God. Or maybe not forsaken by God. At least not entirely. Forsaken by God and the world, but not by hope – which suddenly wafts across the stage, a striking blast of violin air.

On the stage Levadski discovers the tubby figure of

a violinist and cautiously now does take a look through the opera glasses. Where the violinist was sitting a moment ago now sits a harpist, whose gracefulness, Levadski thinks, is not even marred by her ungainly instrument. The caged little bird peers through the stringed window of her dungeon straight into Levadski's binoculars. That's the way I like women, Levadski thinks, tame and sweet in a cage, happy and content. A feast for the eyes beside that liverwurst on the violin. And the clarinet wobbles its head excessively. Female ambition, the curse of humanity, unfortunately also to be found in a lot of men. The conductor, thank God, appears to be totally unaffected by it. Or he has forgotten its allure in the heat of battle, more likely. After all, the fourth movement is a highly complex execution scene ...

Solemn, gloomy marching sounds fill the air of the auditorium. The infatuated lover strangles his beloved and is led to the place of execution. In a moment there will be a bloodbath. Levadski steals a glance at Mr. Witzturn and is horrified to find that his lower lip appears to be taking on a life of its own.

"I love older conductors," Levadski whispers into Mr. Witzturn's ear, "because they are too hard-boiled to boil over and they have left the coquetry of youth behind them. This allows the heart of the music to pulsate, the idea to bud, the essence to become matter." Mr. Witzturn agrees in silence.

Oh, he has fallen asleep again! To confirm the obvious, Mr. Witzturn's head impishly slips to one side, and his lips begin to nibble at an invisible bundle of hay. A disgrace, thinks Levadski, if he misses the last part with the infernal *Dies Irae*. "Mr. Witzturn, Mr. Witzturn!"

Mr. Witzturn doesn't want to hear anything. His head is orbiting in a sphere not unlike that of the music. He effortlessly ascends one cloud mountain after the other, gracefully, light-heartedly. As a sign of his contempt for everything earthly his snoring is soft at first, then it swells to a roll of thunder mingling with the ringing of the death bells in the Golden Hall of the *Musikverein*. The bells ring softer and softer for the executed infatuated lover. Mr. Witzturn's snoring grows louder and louder. "Zzzzzz ...," and he repeats more forcefully "ZZZZZZZZ ..."

Searing looks once again eat their way through the protective crust of darkness in the direction of Levadski's ground floor box. Levadski feels naked, exposed to the most evil thoughts of strangers. But suddenly he no longer feels bothered, seated beside him is a sleeping fellow being who is even more defenseless than he is, someone Levadski has invited to a concert and whose ticket he paid for. We have a right to snore, thinks Levadski, crossing his arms in front of his chest. A knight, a servant, a vassal.

Show your power, fate! We are not masters of ourselves!

Where did he read that? In a monograph? Let the Pharisees cast their poisonous glances. Two old men in the security of their expensive box awaken the wrath of humanity which music is called upon to make fraternal. Take this kiss for all the world. Let them spit poison, the petty-minded. I am a rock in this storm and beside me – Levadski glances over at Mr. Witzturn, whose head is insensibly rocking back and forth on a thin stem in the gathering wind – and beside me a human being! The drop of the executioner's axe, the witches' rabble and scornful laughter are nothing but the common magic of sound, and yet I would like to know where this wind blows from. Why isn't it sweeping the poisoned dwarves from their seats when I have to cling to my chair, Levadski thinks. In the meantime the sound of Mr. Witzturn's snoring has reached a volume surpassing the clamorous commotion of the kettledrums and trumpets.

"What an imposition! Well, I never!"

"Throw the children out!"

"Where is the management!"

"Plebs in the audience."

"Probably foreigners."

Spurred on by all the attention, Mr. Witzturn is now in a snoring competition with the subterraneous stomach rumbling of the double basses. Snore in peace, my friend, Levadski thinks, I will hold the fort. I will take the enemy fire.

Levadski lies down on the floor of the box. From below, the armchairs look like tables, thinks Levadski. Mr. Witzturn is the mountain threatening to capsize onto the prophet. His snoring comes thick and fast, hesitates, falters and then assumes oratorical dimensions again. Cannonballs fly past Levadski, but he does not allow himself to be misled by them. Distant explosions rock the arch of the box. I will protect you, comrade, Levadski thinks, I will protect you … I was once ashamed that I never lay in a trench. And then, Levadski closes his eyes, and then the time came when I had to be ashamed that I'd once been proud for never having lain there. But now I am holding the fort, Mr. Wrumwitz, also lying down …

"Mr. Levadski! It is morning."

"Morning?"

"No, I am only joking, it is," Mr. Witzturn looks at his watch, "10:11, and the concert is over."

"The view is odd."

"It is odd because you are lying on the floor. Wait, I will give you a hand. You lay down when I was offering frenetic applause to the superb conductor, and to the orchestra too, of course, and the blessed composer. As I had my hands full, I could not devote myself to you, you will forgive me."

When Mr. Witzturn seizes Levadski under the arms

and helps him to his feet, Levadski can feel Mr. Witz-turn's alarmingly prominent ribcage through the cloth of his suit.

"We should eat a little something now," Levadski suggests.

"Yes," Mr. Witzturn agrees, fighting for breath, "I am hungry too, music makes you hungrier than sea air."

4
Zimmer / Room 401–441

"NICE TO BE IN THE FRESH AIR AGAIN!" MR. WITZTURN'S
walking stick clatters over the black, wet pavement in
agreement. Two old men shuffle along beside each other
for a while, on the lookout for steps and cracks in the
asphalt ahead of them.

"Once I tripped over a paper cup and broke my hip,"
Levadski says, breaking the silence.

"You can laugh about it?" Mr. Witzturn asks. "How is
that even possible? A paper cup is not an anvil!"

"Yes," Levadski giggles, "lost in thought, I must have
taken the paper cup for something bigger. I became frightened of the thing and just before stumbling properly, I
simply fell over."

"You really are something," smirks Mr. Witzturn, "a
frightened little rabbit. Calcium and egg whites rich in
phosphates is all I can say."

"What good is that for me?"

"Bones as hard as steel," Mr. Witzturn says, sneezing
with a wild squeak into the back of a woman wearing a fur
coat, who immediately hastens her step. "I know what I
am talking about," he continues, "osteoarthritis, titanium
hip joint, complications and this stick." Mr. Witzturn

comes to a halt and swings his walking aid several times close to the side mirror of a parked car. "I would have been spared all this if I had paid attention to the results of medical research and to vitamin D in my diet."

"So, you believe in a healthy diet?"

"He who believes, will be blessed," Mr. Witzturn laughs. "Oh, the revolving door won't move!"

"Push harder. It was working when we left the hotel. Or let me have a go." Levadski leans against the door. Nothing stirs.

"Hhm, perhaps counter-clockwise?" Mr. Witzturn suggests.

"Nothing," Levadski sighs, "perhaps reception has closed?"

"Nonsense, it is not even eleven o'clock. Oh, someone is coming!"

"Please enter through the side door, gentlemen," beckons the dark figure of the concierge. "Unfortunately we have a power outage in the neighborhood." His colleague at the reception desk is waving two greenish glow sticks.

"What are those?"

"They are glow sticks, Professor." The green moon-face belongs to the head concierge who greeted Levadski on the day of his arrival by addressing him as Gracious Sir. "Just give a quick twist here and you get five to six hours of light."

"We are all as green as bog people," Mr. Witzturn remarks with a sense of satisfaction, receiving his light rod.

"Unfortunately the elevator is out of service." The head concierge softly jangles the room keys. "Perhaps the gentlemen would like to take a drink at the bar and then," he gestures vaguely in the direction of the stairs, "go to their rooms."

"Go or ride?" Levadski wants to know.

"We are doing what we can, Professor."

"I didn't know that you were a professor," says Mr. Witzturn, following the light rod of the younger concierge in the direction of the Bar Maria Theresia.

"Well, yes," Levadski says in defense, "what can I say ..." Mr. Witzturn starts giggling again. Strange, Levadski thinks, it's been a while since we had that sparkling wine in the intermission, he can't be drunk. And in no time he finds himself at the bar, bathed in delicate piano music and the chatter of other hotel guests. After the concierge has greeted the piano player across the room with a nod, he wishes Mr. Witzturn and Mr. Levadski a pleasant evening. His light rod swaying in front of him shows him the way back.

"It is very warm in here," Mr. Witzturn remarks.

"Not surprising," Levadski shrugs his shoulders, "with all the burning candles. It's as bright as day."

"Almost," adds Mr. Witzturn, clambering onto a barstool. "I never sit at the bar. The chairs are too high and dangerous for me, but today, I thought, today it feels right."

With a death-defying balancing act Levadski seats himself next to Mr. Witzturn. "I have hung my stick on the rim of the bar," Mr. Witzturn continues. After several failed attempts Levadski's drinking stick stays hanging beside Mr. Witzturn's.

"An elegant rim," says Levadski, discreetly examining Mr. Witzturn's stick through his magnifying glass, "padded with leather at the bottom, did you notice that? Specially for guests with worn out kneecaps." The knob must be made of a tree root or a bulbous nose, thinks Levadski, putting the magnifying glass down on the counter, satisfied. There is no doubt that his drinking stick is more beautiful.

The barman hands the gentlemen two open drink

menus. "Recommend something to us," Levadski says.

"We're game for anything," Mr. Witzturn says, distorting his face into a pathetic grimace. He closes his eyes and sneezes. The hum of the hotel guests disappears for a second but the imperturbable bar pianist, who seems to be playing louder than ever at this precise moment, jumps in alarm, discounts the possibility of a shooting, and, hunching over, continues to play.

"Imperial fruit vodka would be my recommendation." The bartender is propping himself up with both hands on the sink.

"Sounds very refreshing. It is exactly what we need in this heat, isn't it, Mr. Witzturn?" Mr. Witzturn agrees.

"Game for anything," he repeats, giving a wink and deliberating whether he should sneeze again.

"I will hold on to the glasses," the bartender smiles.

"Nope, it's not going to happen," Mr. Witzturn declares resignedly, after having listened intently to his insides. Levadski breathes a sigh of relief.

"Haaaaaa!" Mr. Witzturn starts roaring. "Haaaa-haaa-haaa-tchoo," he drily continues, opening his eyes.

"Bless you," a wrinkled lady motions to him from one of the tables, her hand draped in shimmering pearls.

"Thank you," Mr. Wtizturn replies from atop the high lookout of his barstool. "Haaaa-haaa!" he adds. It is not that embarrassing after all, thinks Levadski. I hope he stops sneezing so we can end the evening with a nice little conversation.

"Cheerio," Mr. Witzturn mumbles into his glass.

"Yes, cheers," says Levadski gently, taking a decent swig that pleasantly and coolly flows down his throat.

"Do you know why it smells so strongly of alcohol in here?" Mr. Witzturn, with one eye mischievously closed, waits for Levadski's reply. "You think it is because of all the bottles that are lined up on the bar shelf?"

Who Is Martha?

"I don't know, perhaps a bottle broke. Evaporation?"

"It is indeed, my dear Mr. Levadski, because of evaporation, but from all the old farts sitting at the tables," Mr. Witzturn whispers and begins to snort.

When he stinks of schnapps himself, Levadski thinks, raising his glass. "I drink to ..." Levadski deliberates, he wants to say something poetic, something succinct and uplifting. "I drink to the kindness of humanity!"

"Bravo!" croaks a woman's hoarse voice from one of the tables near the piano. To be on the safe side, the piano player intimates a bow, even if he knows it was not directed at his virtuosity. In revenge, he begins to hammer out a dramatic song.

"You are a poet," Mr. Witzturn sighs, taking another sip and rubbing his chest with a circular motion through his shirt. "Paahh, vodka is good for the arteries ..." In Mr. Witzturn's eyes the bottles of cognac, whiskey and vodka on the bar shelf glow like molten lava. Candles flicker in the bellies of the bottles and their reflections rotate in a circle dance around Levadski's bald head.

Levadski slowly leans back, wondering where the backrest has gone. "A barstool does not have a backrest," the hunched figure of Mr. Witzturn beside him informs him. Levadski stops himself, eyes wide. "Let me treat you to a second vodka," Mr. Witzturn announces in the direction of the bartender.

"Two fruit vodkas for the gentlemen," the bartender says to himself and disappears into the small dark connecting room.

"To your health!" Mr. Witzturn, his glass raised, waits for Levadski.

"To you, Mr. Witzturn." Levadski hastily finishes his old glass and reaches for the new one filled to the brim.

"It doesn't matter," Levadski says turning to Mr. Witzturn, "in what form we encounter beauty." Mr. Witzturn slowly turns his head. His eyes are dull, tired, as if he were pleading for mercy, that's how Mr. Witzturn looks through Levadski. "The moment and the connection in which we experience that beauty are also irrelevant," Levadski goes on. "We should not let ourselves be confused by the recurrence and arbitrariness of beauty. For it is … it is," Levadski repeats a little more softly.

"It is what?" Mr. Witzturn asks, after blinking several times. Levadski doesn't know.

He is suddenly scared of tackling the thankless subject.

"Perhaps beauty is just the certainty that you don't need memory of it in order to be certain of it," Levadski replies, almost inaudibly and falls silent, which doesn't seem to bother Mr. Witzturn.

"We are good at being silent," Levadski says to Mr. Witzturn a moment later. "But one of us is more deeply silent than the other. Just as in a conversation there is always one person who talks more than the other. When somebody speaks, a story is being told and someone is listening. And when there is silence?"

Levadski looks at Mr. Witzturn's hand, which absent-mindedly allows itself to be bitten by a nut in a silver bowl.

"When it comes to silence, there is keeping silent and concealing," Mr. Witzturn replies.

"What are you concealing from me?"

"Excuse me?"

"I mean, did you want to tell me something?"

"When you started so euphorically to writhe on the floor of the box during the concert, I remembered a person I have not thought of in a long time," Mr. Witzturn says, looking up at the ceiling.

"Well, during the concert I thought of my piano teacher. He must be dead now for at least eighty years. He was already an old man at the time. But as perky as a pickle. Once I arrived at my piano lesson and started to play a piece. I was hunched and tense, I was expecting a shower of abuse any second. But something else happened. My piano teacher just tipped out of his armchair and was suddenly in a better world, without having wasted a word. A dull thud. Do you know what it sounds like when a head hits a parquet floor?"

Levadski shakes his head.

"It makes a pleasant sound, it is all but hollow."

Mr. Witzturn is stirring a little Chinese umbrella in his glass. "It was only when I heard that thud that the tension in my shoulders disappeared, and I could play. I could fly. I could embrace the world."

"I understand," Levadski mumbles.

"Of course I was sad, I was scared, and suddenly alone with the music, the secret of which I was at the time beginning to divine. My God, I felt wretched at that moment. Yet something inside me was rejoicing: a person had died; a person whom I admired had breathed his last, in my presence, while I was sitting at his piano. Do you understand what that means?"

"Yes. Ahem," Levadski clears his throat.

"My piano teacher did not say a word and still left a message for me in his silence. A secret. You understand?"

"Yes." Levadski has a herring standing on one leg in his throat.

"And so," Mr. Witzturn continues, "and so I remembered this man during the concert. Now I know what an enormous role this silence played in my life. Oh!" Mr. Witzturn bursts out laughing, "what a remarkable person he was, I can see him before me. When I consider that this figure, for so long, for such an unspeakable length of time, failed to touch the surface of my memory, as if he had existed in an earlier or different life, but barely in my own. Oh," Mr. Witzturn slowly shakes his head, "if your concert hadn't …"

"And now in honor of the two gentlemen at the bar," the voice of the piano player can be heard saying, "the most beautiful song in the world!"

Ochi chernyyyyye. *Dum dum dum.*
Ochi strastnyyyyye
Ochi zhguchiye i prekrasnye. *Convulsion.*
Kak lyublyu ya vas!
Kak, *hit the keys*, boyus' ya vas!
Znat', uvidel vas ya v nedobryi chas!

"What does that mean?" Mr. Witzturn is pulling Levadski's sleeve.

"The most beautiful song in the world. *Black Eyes.* Do you know it?"

"I vaguely remember it."

"In which case, take my magnifying glass," Levadski orders.

"Don't put it to your eye!" Levadski guides the magnifying glass in Mr. Witzturn's hand towards his right ear. "Right, and now focus on the song!" Levadski slips off his barstool.

"Where are you going?" Mr. Witzturn exclaims, holding the magnifying glass to his ear, a sound of slight dismay in his voice.

"I am seizing the opportunity, so long as it's still dark in the room!" says Levadski. His laughter is drowned out by the applause of the bar guests who seem to have considerably increased in number in the space of two glasses of vodka.

"*Ochi chernye*, if you would be so kind," Levadski whispers in the withering ear of the piano player. The piano player nods and drops his fingers on the keys.

Des yeux noirs, des yeux pleins de passion!
Des yeux ravageurs et sublimes!

Goodness, thinks Levadski, never before have I sung in public, not even to myself, and now at the end of my days I am singing in a foreign language and swinging my hips like a female long-tailed tit.

Comme je vous aime, comme j'ai peur de vous!
Je sais, je vous ai vus, pas au bon moment!

Levadski, his gaze directed upwards, puts a hand to his chest as if wanting to stop his heart, his life and the course of time, to let the moment linger!

Pas au bon moment ...

... He hurls the lyrics gently towards the ceiling, clenching his fist that a moment ago had been resting on his heart. His life is pulsating inside it.

"Bravoooo!" This is what Levadski has been waiting for. Relieved, he unclenches his fist and lets his life flutter into the room and do a little business on the heads of all the audience. Unnoticed, it returns to its master and slips into his left trouser leg.

"*Salto! Salto! Salto!*" chants the audience, urging him on.

"Please, Professor!" Levadski hears from the bar. Who was that? The bartender or Mr. Witzturn? A white spitz is sitting stiffly on Levadski's barstool. Levadski's stick in its muzzle, it seems desperate to go for a walk.

"I'll be quick!" Levadski calls out to the dog. "Sit!" he adds, and with thrashing arms climbs onto a one-legged table. I hope the dog does not eat my expensive drinking stick, thinks Levadski, and besides, the shards of the glass tubing could damage his stomach. Who would be liable for that?

"*Salto! Salto!*" the bar guests slur cheerfully in Levadski's direction.

"*Olé!*" Levadski, his hand raised and index finger outstretched, requests silence. He looks over at the bar again. The spitz seems to have grown, not just in height but in breadth too, and is now standing, leaning on Levadski's stick, a silent threat in front of the barstool. It is not the pursed mocking muzzle that irritates Levadski, not the whistling that he thinks he can perceive, it is something else. What is it? "God almighty!" Levadski shouts, teetering on the table, "there is a ray of sunlight growing out of the dog's ear! It's pointing at me!"

Come on, shake your body baby, do the conga,
I know you can't control yourself any longer,

... the piano player sings, winking at Levadski.

Come on, shake your body baby, do the conga,
I know you can't control yourself any longer,

"What shall I do?"
"Dance! Show the mutt you're busy!" the piano player whispers, while he hammers the keys like he was born to do it. "Maybe then he'll go for a walk on his own."

Come on, shake your body baby, do the conga,
I know you can't control yourself any longer,
Feel the rhythm of the music getting stronger,
Don't you fight it 'til you tried it, do the conga beat.

Levadski is on the table flailing his arms again. "Not like that," the piano player growls, "otherwise the dog will

Who Is Martha?

think you're drowning and he'll try to rescue you."

Everybody gather 'round now,
Let your body feel the heat.
Don't you worry if you can't dance,
Let the music move your feet.

Levadski wriggles his behind and traces zeros in the air
with his palms. When he throws a cautious glance at the
bar, the silver knob of his stick in the vodka glass stabs
him in the eye. "The dog is gone!" he shouts at the piano
player, who wistfully brings the song to a close.

It's the rhythm of the island
And like sugarcane so sweet,
If you want to do the conga
You've got to listen to the beat.

"Thank you, you saved me." Levadski, still standing
on the table, shakes the piano player's hand.
"You are welcome," he smiles, and a white curl falls
out of his mouth.
The dog! shoots through Levadski's mind. In order to
gain a few moments, Levadski asks the piano player for
the time. His mouth twists itself into a smile again. Levadski desperately tries to think what it is that he actually
wants to gain time for.
"I – don't – wear – a – watch," the piano player says.
With every word another curl of hair flutters out of his
mouth. Weak-kneed, Levadski returns to the bar. His di-
version tactic is still a mystery to him.
"Well danced, Professor," Mr. Witzturn, who is now
back, says in praise. His head is a dog's head, his body
is Levadski's drinking stick, inside which a dark liquid is
rising and falling.

"Stop the thief!" Levadski hears himself call, while his dentures take on a life of their own and leap from his mouth. With a smacking sound they bite through Mr. Witzturn's waist, which is made of glass.

"Mr. Levadski, hello! Your bread is getting warm."

"Sorry, I drifted off for a moment."

"Microsleep can be dangerous for drivers and people sitting at the bar." Mr. Witzturn scrutinizes Levadski with a tired smile. "You didn't miss much. We are still sitting here without electricity, isn't that so, maestro?"

"The guests are slowly getting nervous," the bartender observes, filling several glasses with vodka. "Everybody would like to be in their rooms, but nobody dares to go to the upper floors in the dark."

"The steps can be fatal." Mr. Witzturn's forefinger ascends an imaginary spiral staircase. "One step too many or too few, and you are in paradise. Not a certainty of course," he adds after taking a generous swig from his glass.

"Tell me about your piano teacher instead!" Levadski bids him.

"You know …" Mr. Witzturn says, closing his eyes. "Oh, it's such a long time ago." Mr. Witzturn forces open his eyes again and turns toward Levadski's barstool. His gaze staggers over Levadski's face, like after a thousand-year sleep. "This evening during the concert I remembered a dead man, and suddenly … oh, everything is unspeakable!" Mr. Witzturn repeats.

"And suddenly?"

"And suddenly for the first time in my life I am sure that I have lived."

"Oh, Mr. Witzturn," Levadski pulls a crumpled handkerchief from his trousers. A family of dust bunnies has used the darkness of his trouser pocket in order to multiply shamelessly. Their wool bodies are soft.

"Oh, Mr. Witzturn, don't say a thing like that, you are alive. Still alive."

"Just a memory," Mr. Witzturn shakes his head, "a single memory, resurrected as if by magic, is sufficient for answering all questions, for airing all secrets that have tormented you, you understand?"

Levadski places a hand on the cool glass of Mr. Witzturn's wristwatch.

"A single memory appears to be sufficient in order to close the circle of life," Mr. Witzturn says, carefully withdrawing his hand. He pulls a checked handkerchief with a large ink spot from his suit trousers. Levadski wrestles with himself for a few seconds before deciding it is best not to point out the ink spot to Mr. Witzturn, so as not to disconcert him.

"This evening my life has come full circle," Mr. Witzturn says, wiping a tear of pity from his left and then his right eye. "I have, if you like, been liberated."

"Let's drink to it!" says Levadski, vigorously blowing his nose, in which nothing worth mentioning is to be found.

"Lucky you!" Mr. Witzturn smiles. With his inky eyes he looks as if he had been hit with a potato masher. "I wish I could blow my nose like you." Mr. Witzturn taps his plastic nose three times.

"Touch wood," Levadski jokes.

"Well," Mr. Witzturn continues, "my piano player was an eccentric old man. If he were sitting here at the bar, here between the two of us," Mr. Witzturn brushes his hand over the impressive hunchback of the absent man, "if he were here, he could easily be taken for our son. I mean for one of our sons," Mr. Witzturn corrects himself.

"You mean the son of one of us," Levadski gently corrects him.

"For our mutual son," Mr. Witzturn stresses. "While we are on the subject of it, what role do biological parents play?"

"By all means." Levadski presses a hand to his chest, while making a dismissive gesture with the other.

"At some point," Mr. Witzturn whispers, "you are so free, so high, so …" – his eyes of India ink scan the ceiling – "so, how should I put it, hhmm. Where was I?"

"Your piano teacher," Levadski comes to the rescue.

"Yes, my piano teacher sometimes had the habit of naming the piece being played after hearing only a few bars. How often we went to concerts together. I was a flourishing meadow of pimples, my master an elegant devil. Nothing was too difficult for him. Not even the most obscure compositions. He knew them all. As if he had written them himself." Mr. Witzturn gives a snort and mops his brow with the ink-stained handkerchief. "His hearing was as remarkable as his tonal memory and his knowledge of compositions. He could isolate every single instrument from even the most boisterous orchestral clamor. While I contentedly devoted myself to the music, he would say, That's all very well, but the clarinet played G sharp instead of F."

"Unbelievable." Levadski is amazed and slides back and forth on his barstool several times.

"The best thing," Mr. Witzturn slaps his hand on the bar, "ha-ha-ha! The best thing … ho-ho-ho," Mr. Witzturn is rocking on his seat, "was his spyglass. It was a heavy Victorian telescope that my piano teacher was in the habit of taking to concerts. Perhaps my imagination is deceiving me now, but I could swear it was a telescope."

"How eccentric!" It warms the cockles of Levadski's heart. "A telescope!"

"Or an ear trumpet, hm, one of the two." Mr. Witzturn's eyebrows shoot up. "Of course it was a telescope!

We mostly sat right at the front, in the wrong seats. This was of no consequence to my piano teacher. If someone arrived who had the right tickets he would be sent away with the words, 'Look for another seat, you don't know anything about music anyway.'"

"Delightful!" Levadski taps his thighs. To be on the safe side I am getting off the barstool, just in case he gets more amusing, he thinks, placing his feet on the ground.

"And then," Mr. Witzturn sprays Levadski's eye with spittle, "from one of the front rows, my piano teacher would stare through his very conspicuous instrument at the virtuoso's fingers, embarrassing the poor man completely. After being dealt the devastating blow of 'Wrong!' he would then turn as white as a sheet. 'Wrong' and 'Bad,' he would mostly add, and that was that."

"What do you mean, that was that?" Levadski asks, doubled over with laughter.

"Well," Mr. Witzturn smirks, "he made them all uneasy that way. Anybody who remained practiced on the quiet, until they really could play. Play elegantly, as if they were drinking a glass of water. The more difficult and unplayable a piece in the music was, the faster and more easily a survivor like that would play it."

"What happened to the others?"

"The others were unable to cope with the unreasonable demands of my piano teacher, I assume. No loss, God forgive me. Anyone who like a shrinking violet sways in the wind of great art ought to jump in the lake!"

"After us the Flood" Levadski says, holding on to the chair leg, or is it one of Mr. Witzturn's legs? Like an ark on the high seas, thinks Levadski, an ark without passengers. An ark in a world without animals and human beings. The plants will survive us. It is said that mushrooms grow for years on the ocean floor without sunlight.

Sailor, stop dreaming …

"The pianist has risen," Mr. Witzturn whispers in Levadski's ear.

… don't think of home.
Sailor, wind and waves
Are calling you.

"Well, he needs to keep the guests in a good mood," Levadski remarks yawning. "There will be some guests who have fallen asleep in their dark corner, won't there?" Instead of moving his head, Mr. Witzturn rolls his eyes as far as they will go to one side. Like two billiard balls on a sinking ship. "In the dark, it is difficult to see who is sleeping and who is squinty-eyed by nature," he mumbles. "Maestro, how about a ladies' cocktail for the two of us?"

Your home is the ocean,
Your friends are the stars
Over Rio and Shanghai,
Over Bali and Hawaii.

"What's that?"
"I was just telling the maestro that you would like something syrupy, a ladies' drink, for a change."
"With pleasure, if you will join me."
"Would the gentlemen like to take a look at the cocktail menu?" the barman opens a leather folder.
"We can't see anything," Mr. Witzturn laughs, "even less than we could two hours ago."

Your love is your ship.
Your yearning is the distance.

Who Is Martha?

And only to them are you faithful
For a lifetime.

"Something syrupy," the bartender says, "I am just
thinking about what would complement the fruit vodka
the gentlemen have already drunk."

Sailor, stop dreaming.
Don't think of me,
Sailor, for the unknown
Already awaits you.

"Just mix up something for us," Mr. Witzturn
requests.
"Any old thing isn't suitable for sophisticated consumption!" Levadski remarks in a reproachful voice.
"Is that so?" Mr. Witzturn menacingly asks the bartender, who nods in agreement.
"A bartender, however, would never lecture his guests,"
Levadski remarks. "After all, a bar has a cultural and social
function, hasn't it?" The bartender agrees with Levadski
again. Mr. Witzturn, piqued, rolls his eyes.

Your home is the ocean,
Your friends are the stars
Over Rio and Shanghai,
Over Bali and Hawaii.

"Just mix up something for us," Mr. Witzturn starts in
all over again.
"My God!" Levadski touches his brow. "Any old thing
will neither do for us, nor will it do in the eyes of the young
man whose care we are in. Get that into your head!"
"Something syrupy for ladies," Mr. Witzturn adds.
"Let the man in charge of the bar have his say. What

cocktails have you got anyway?"

"Would the gentlemen like to know exactly what we have got? We have," the barman looks at Levadski and the coughing Mr. Witzturn in turn, "a large selection of bases, each embracing a large choice of cocktails. We have," he pinches his eyes, "aperitifs, classic drinks, low alcohol drinks, non-alcoholic drinks, hot drinks, drinks for hangovers and corpse-reviving cocktails ..."

Your love is your ship.
Your yearning is the distance.
And only to them are you faithful
For a lifetime.

"... Martini cocktails, sours, juleps, highballs, flips, fizzes, coladas, to mention a few. Then we have the spirit-based cocktails ..."

"For example?" Mr. Witzturn asks, yawning widely, as if wanting to spit out an entire egg. A similar-sized egg slips out of Levadski's mouth. At the last moment he manages to hide this embarrassment behind a fist.

"No, we really are interested," Mr. Witzturn explains, "aren't we, Mr. Levadski?"

"Tell us about the spirit bases, please, if you would," Levadski asks, stifling a second yawn.

"For example, Campari drinks are mixed with a spirit base, I am sure the gentlemen know that."

"Yes, when you go into a café in summer, you frequently see fogged-over Campari glasses in the hands of older ladies, don't you, Mr. Levadski?"

"I seldom go out, especially when it is very hot." He should leave off saying 'don't you, Mr. Levadski,' Levadski thinks; if he says it once more, I am going to tell him.

"Campari and orange was already a classic before our time – Costa Brava, Bella Donna, Bella Musica, Bella

Bella." Mr. Witzturn is gently swaying on his barstool, on and on, even when he can't think of any more Bellas.

"And then there are also other Campari drinks," the bartender cautiously continues, "Cardinal, Rosita, Negroni ..."

"What other cocktails are there on the planet? Enlighten us, young man," Levadski says, turning to the bartender who, according to the rules of the art, has been polishing a glass the entire time.

"Vodka drinks, for example, although nowadays they are more often drunk neat," replies the bartender, dipping a cocktail glass in a basin of water. "Many people drink spirits neat out of reverence for the drink. I too would probably never mix particular spirits. Gin and vodka or gin and whisky. God forbid."

"Gin really is something special," Mr. Witzturn yawns down the length of his flowery tie.

"A bar without gin," the bartender comes into his own, "is like an eagle without feathers. You can do anything with it."

"Game for anything," Mr. Witzturn mumbles, letting his chin sink onto his chest.

"No other spirit has created so many classics," the barman continues, "Pink Gin, Gin and Tonic, or Martini Dry, would not exist without gin. The more recent hugely popular Alexander's Sister cocktail wouldn't either."

"What is so special about gin?" Levadski's chin is also seeking purchase on the lower floors of his upper body.

"If I were on a desert island," says the bartender, "and I had to decide on a single alcohol base in order to mix drinks, I would choose gin. Why? Because gin is easy, down-to-earth, discreet, soft. It is self-sufficient. It is self-confident and doesn't need any external endorsement, that is to say, it needs no other alcohol."

"The self is the man," drones Mr. Witzturn, his chin

on his chest like a schnitzel rolling in flour.

What would you be doing on a desert island as a head bartender? Levadski can't vouch for whether he said these words or Mr. Witzturn said them. Perhaps, he thinks, I was only thinking out loud. Or I only whispered, very softy whispered ... a deserted bar, but why on an island?

"Never mix gin with vodka, gin with rum, gin with brandy," he hears the bartender whispering into the glasses.

"What did you say?"

"Whisky with liqueurs, gin with juice, vermouth with gin, gin with tequila, juice bitters ... A bar without an island is like a bar without glasses." The bartender's monologue is a sigh, a rustling in the wind.

The white jacket flutters like a thousand leaves in the wind, thinks Levadski, white poplar ...

"Gin appears to be an ingenious chap," Mr. Witzturn purrs. Levadski closes one eye. Or maybe he opens it? Inward or outward. This thought does not torment him for long either.

"Lone Tree for example, very popular with the ladies, gin, dry vermouth, red vermouth, a drop of orange bitters, stirred on ice, served up to the old clapperclaws in a martini glass."

"Hahaha," Mr. Witzturn grunts, to the accompaniment of the sound of his creaking barstool. "Clapperclaws, I will remember that!" Mr. Witzturn learns the new word as he snores. Entire forests are felled with the axe of his nose.

"Or Flying Dutchman, timeless, simply timeless. Mix gin with an eighth of lime and ice, throw it out the window, done."

"Or!" the bartender's voice is attacking Levadski's nervous system, "the Merry Widow Number One!"

Who Is Martha?

"Number One?" Mr. Witzturn asks, taken aback. Levadski puts his hand to his chest. His dentures are still resting in his mouth. Don't sleep, he commands himself, don't bat an eyelid.

"Merry Widow is still a cocktail that many gentlemen like to order for their female company. Dry vermouth, a few squirts of Benedictine and orange bitters, a drop of anisette, gin and a fat lemon, stirred in a mixing beaker and strained into the precooled female countenance. Pure seduction."

"I'm for drinking neat," Mr. Witzturn whispers.

The bartender clears his throat. Flying Dutchman is what he would recommend for the gentlemen. Not a syrupy drink, but by all means suitable for ladies. Clear and sleek, soaring flight, sharp descent.

The gentlemen agree.

"I am extremely interested in your piano teacher. When I try and imagine him, I can almost imagine what it is like to lose one's mind," Levadski admits. Mr. Witzturn starts rubbing his eyes again.

"I don't understand what you mean."

"Suddenly it was as if I were you and your piano teacher were giving me a piano lesson, not you. And it was I that had told you all the stories you gave me the pleasure of listening to this evening."

"I don't understand." Mr. Witzturn loses several invisible eyelashes as he continues rubbing his eyes. "What difference does it make whether you knew my piano teacher or I knew him? He is dead. That's the only thing that counts."

"I hope not," says Levadski, "I hope not, Mr. Witzturn, we know him, and that should count."

"Your cocktails, gentlemen." Levadski is elated.

"How beautifully you have prepared the Flying Dutchman!"

"He knew his music," Mr. Witzturn says and drinks, without looking Levadski in the eye, "my piano teacher."

"He still knows his music," Levadski reassures him after a lengthy pause. "Now he is no longer a medium for you, but you are one yourself."

"You are a poet," Mr. Witzturn tries to joke. The soul of a shy male dog barks out from inside him. "You may very well be right. After all, my piano teacher was a devotee of Scriabin. Do you know Scriabin? Scriabin's desire was not only to be one with the music, but also for music to merge with all the senses. Do you know Scriabin?"

Levadski nods. A desire tickles his throat, the desire to bark, softly, very quietly and unobtrusively. Scriabin is dead, too.

"His idea of absolute music was unique. Scriabin worked on a composition that he programmatically called *Mysterium*. Here all the arts were to amalgamate into one gigantic *Gesamtkunstwerk*: music, voice, song, dance, color, scent … The performance of this composition was intended to take place in India and throw everything else into the shadow of what even the most opulent operas had ever been able to offer. Do you understand what it means to be a Scriabin," Mr. Witzturn asks, "to be a devotee of Scriabin? That's what my piano teacher was."

"An unfathomable secret," Levadski murmurs, attempting to impale an ice cube in his glass with a stirrer.

"There are at least two things about Scriabin's music that are entirely unusual," Mr. Witzturn carries on. "He started out as a kind of Russian Chopin and ended up by taking giant steps, without running or tripping, at the boundaries of tonality."

"At the boundaries of tonality," Levadski repeats, stirring more rapidly in his glass.

"Scriabin," Mr. Witzturn continues, "never completely said goodbye to Romantic music and a tonal ideal, but broke through many metric, formal and harmonic conventions. This means something, doesn't it? Conventions!" Mr. Witzturn fumbles with a hand that can't decide: should it clench itself into a fist or not?

"My mother," says Levadski, "my mother was my piano teacher, if I may be permitted to call her that. Women like song and dance."

"They are music," Mr. Witzturn grins into his glass. Levadski smiles embarrassedly through the ice cube he has jammed between two straws.

"It is only logical that children die after their parents. Everything you think is laughable or unnecessary as a child, you take seriously and consider important in the end – through the magic of death."

"Magic?" Mr. Witzturn raises an eyebrow. "Very poetic …"

"Yes, magic, it throws a ruthless light on things that are intended to and desire to creep into the lives of those left behind," says Levadski. His straws tremble and the ice cube sinks into the tides of the cocktail. "My mother was my piano teacher," Levadski says, poking around in the hollow of an ice cube. "Her tinkling bothered me for as long as she lived. Her vacant face hovering over the piano and above all the clouds and her sweating, even that gave me a fright. Now I still can't watch the musicians in their ecstasy without feeling horror."

"Of course, you are confronted with the emptiness that the musicians see. The emptiness makes you scared," Mr. Witzturn remarks.

"Exactly, or death that is full of promise. Will you be fulfilled or will you be unfulfilled? My mother seemed to simultaneously decompose, burn, to be reduced to molecules when she was playing music. How could it not be frightening? You know, she sent me on my way with something beautiful, something I took no notice of as a boy. A lesson! Something inside me preserved the moment and put it on a pedestal. This pedestal was to be the resting place of the lesson she secretly imparted to me. Would you like to know what the lesson was?" Woe if he says no, thinks Levadski. He could not offend me more deeply.

Mr. Witzturn nods.

"Does that mean yes or no?"

"I feel like I have been transported back to my youth when I am with you," Mr. Witzturn smiles, "when I was so eager to understand women."

"Yes or no?"

"I underestimated bad habits like Yes or no, Do you really love me, How do I look, and so forth in my youthful megalomania. I always wanted to grasp a woman in her entirety. That was fatal."

"One last time – yes or no?"

"Yes, for God's sake, yes, yes, yes, there is nothing more I long for than to know what the lesson was that your blessed mother taught you!"

"Once my mother drew a comparison to explain how you played a suspension before a chord at the end of a piano piece." Mr. Witzturn asks him to speak up a little. "If I think about it now," Levadski clears his throat, "I can now see that the comparison she drew at the time was to become a metaphor for my little life." Levadski waits in vain for Mr. Witzturn to ask what kind of comparison it was, coughs and carries on: "The piece I was playing was nearing the end, the finish was a soft melancholy minor, but I just wanted to be done and so I played it with equal impatience, something my mother was not at all happy about. Look, she said, up there on the mountain there is a mighty gate in front of a beautiful castle. You are a messenger, riding towards that gate. From a great distance you can hear the old wooden gate snapping shut into its lock. That is the way you are meant to play the suspension."

"To your mother!" Mr. Witzturn raises his glass, bows his head and fortunately only stabs his cheek with his straw. "Only I don't see what the lesson to be learned consists of."

"In the metaphor, Mr. Witzturn, in the metaphor."

"In the metaphor for what? And what does it have to do with your life? A beautiful castle, a gate snapping shut?"

"My little life," Levadski mumbles, "yes, my life, perhaps she wanted to make me the gift of a metaphor, as a greeting, as a dowry for my future, and I, I don't know what ..."

A soft neighing can be heard coming from Mr. Witzturn's chest. His mouth is closed, the corners are pointing at the peanuts that have missed his mouth and are now mostly lying on the floor, crushed. By the light of the candles they look like the bone splinters of tiny skulls.

"Down there," Levadski points to the peanuts, "down there, there are little people. It is grotesque, almost perverse, to deny the existence of gnomes. Fairy tales do not lie. They exist. Down there!"

"Come off it," Mr. Witzturn neighs.

"Don't you notice something?"

"Oh, what!"

"That we are shooting upwards in our chairs? And the earth has after all turned out to be a disc."

"I will have another Cosmonaut Cocktail." Levadski clutches his head. A woman's round face with a crimson pout is sitting on Mr. Witzturn's chair.

"Here I am!"

"Oh, there you are," Levadski breathes with a sigh of relief, "for a moment I lost my bearings and thought you were the young woman who sat down beside me."

"The castle in the distance, the mighty gate, the lock snapping shut, the castle, the gate ...," Mr. Witzturn repeats expectantly.

"Well," Levadski scratches his head. "The metaphor of the castle … hm. I knew it a moment ago. How exasperating," he moans, "a moment ago I knew it, and now, now that I want to talk about it, it has escaped me."

"Fine, another time then," Mr. Witzturn sighs.

"I've got it!"

"Yes?"

"Hhm. A moment ago I had it."

"Should I perhaps explain to you how I see it with the castle and the gate in your life?" Levadski has no objection. Mr. Witzturn blinks a few times and begins to talk.

"Don't be offended, but in my eyes the metaphor of the closing gate seems quite trivial."

"What do you see?" A glob of saliva gets stuck in Levadski's windpipe. He grips fast to the bar while coughing.

"The image of the mighty gate falling shut …" Mr. Witzturn is chewing on his lower lip, "it could be death your blessed mother wanted to prepare you for." Levadski's eyes light up. "And that as a human being you should not be too surprised if you find yourself standing in front of this mighty gate one day." Levadski's cheeks are on fire. "If it was not a lesson, it was definitely a sign, a sign to raise the spirits. From one person to another. Now you have heard it from a stranger. The way you wanted to." Levadski's chin nods and drops to his chest like a wilted leaf on a snow-covered pond. Beneath his shirt, spring arrives. "You know everything yourself …"

"A Cosmonaut Cocktail for the lady."

"How pretty, it even has a sugared lemon slice … A ring of Saturn!" The white face is enchanted.

"A foreigner," in Mr. Witzturn's opinion.

"Like all of us," whispers Levadski.

"I am writing a book about an old man," the young lady with the Cosmonaut Cocktail tells the bartender. "A

Who Is Martha?

lonely old man returns to the city of his childhood in order to die there, so that the circle is complete."

"That sounds like a fascinating story," the bartender says with a frosty expression.

"Here, in this bar," says the pale female cosmonaut, "my hero squanders his wealth, everything he has. That's why I need to try all the cocktails an aged gentleman would order. For example, cocktails that were popular in his youth."

"Allow me to make a remark," the bartender says. "An older gentleman would more likely sit at a table over there by the window or very close to the piano. The bar would not be the place for him."

"A foreigner," Levadski hears Mr. Witzturn mumble. "And still no electricity." Whether I keep my eyes open or closed is really beside the point, thinks Levadski, I am fine. I am fine. Fine …

"It depends on how old the hero of your novel is. For example, a Cosmonaut Cocktail like that would have been popular in the sixties." The bartender appears to be speaking out of a Millésimé champagne bottle.

"I presume," says the young lady, sounding out of a Finlandia bottle, "that my fellow compatriot Gagarin made a contribution towards the naming of the cocktail."

"The first man in space," echoes from the bartender's secret glass cubbyhole.

"She is from the Soviet Union," Mr. Witzturn growls into Levadski's ear, making his lids flutter.

"I don't know," the Russian says, "whether he really was the first man in space."

The Soviet Union doesn't exist anymore, Levadski wants to say to Mr. Witzturn, but to do so he would have to open his eyes. Or his mouth. The bartender's laughter sounds like an explosion of sparkling bubbles.

"But there was nobody out there before your fellow

countryman." Levadski imagines one of the bartender's eyes swimming up the neck of the bottle.

"I don't know," the female cosmonaut repeats stubbornly, "whether Gagarin was the first man in space. Perhaps there were other creatures there long before him. For example, after they decided to leave our planet for particular reasons."

"For what reasons?" the bartender wants to know.

"To give the apes a chance, I would say."

"Clever, very clever," the bartender is amused, "perhaps these apes were meant to follow the example of the first true cosmonauts and give the animals a chance?"

"I plead for the horses," says the Russian. Before we all fly to Mars, we should put the horses in the right light." The bartender finds dogs more exciting. May dogs rule!

"Most of them are overbred," the Russian objects, "and besides, dogs are half human. Too spoiled. Wolves would be better, because," the Russian deliberates, "they are the apes of the dog world."

"May the wolves populate our cities," the bartender cheers, "drive our cars! May ..."

"A clear-thinking wolf would keep its paws off our civilization," Mr. Witzturn interrupts. The bartender places his hand on the shaker. It immediately fogs up, and he remains in that position, sucking in his lips. A veil of perfume wafts into Levadski's face.

"A dense forest with ivy, ferns and mosses, of course," the Russian replies, "that would be a wolf civilization." Mr. Witzturn laughs.

"The forests are dying! I am afraid your wolf will have to learn to drive our cars."

"It will not do so under duress," the Russian counters, "it will carry out its business on the arid land until a magnificent forest carpets over it, even if it has to give its life in return!"

A true poet, thinks Levadski.

"Gimlet, Hot Toddy, Americano, Mai Thai," the bartender hisses, as if he were enflamed in wild hatred against the cocktails. "Bourbon Highball, Harvey Wallbanger, Sours, White and Black Russian, to summarize. Very popular in the sixties: Pimm's Cocktail, Screwdriver, Mojito, Milk Punch, Vodka was newly discovered. To have a bar at home also became fashionable at that time."

"I remember," Mr. Witzturn croaks, "the stiff cocktail parties where I stood until I was ready to drop and religiously kissed housewives' moisturized hands. Hungry and dazed, I bit into their sausage fingers and scratched my mouth on their precious stone rings. There was nothing to eat, just masses of cocktails mixed by the gentleman of the house. That's the way we created the foundation for our own conservation, isn't that so Mr., er ..." Levadski smiles at Mr. Witzturn through closed eyes. "I was never a party animal, Mr., er ..."

"I suggest we drink a cocktail from our youth. Maestro!" Mr. Witzturn says in a weak voice. "What did they drink during the war?"

"In wartime there was no time for sophisticated drinking," Levadski interjects.

"Then let's drink something from the sixties." The bartender recommends Cuba Libre. Lime, white rum, Coke and a Caribbean zest for life.

"I'll pass," says Mr. Witzturn, twiddling a bent straw between his fingers, "to me Cuba Libre sounds like a disrespectful belittlement of revolutionary ideals."

"But my dear Mr. Witzturn, the time of revolutions is over. At least it is for us."

"Once more you are mistaken, dear Mr. Levadski. Nobody should underestimate revolution's contribution to the improvement of the decline of the world, nor should we. We are ..."

Mr. Witzturn scratches his temple as if in so doing new ideas could trickle out. "There is no doubt that we are on the verge of a new revolution."

"Strange," Levadski shrugs his shoulders, "I am not sensing anything of this revolution."

"Not surprising," Mr. Witzturn laughs hoarsely. "It is a subtle revolution, one the people really need."

"Which people?"

"In the first instance, our occidental people. Oh," Mr. Witzturn purses his lips in pleasure, "a Romantic age is dawning, the time of the Neoromantics, an age that will make the Enlightenment and the embarrassing turbulence of the last century seem like a bundle of dried forest mushrooms."

"Fantastic." Levadski folds his hands as if he were about to say a prayer at table.

"The revolution is creeping on," Mr. Witzturn adds solemnly. "We will have to dress warmly for it."

"Is there a different cocktail with Caribbean zest for life?" Levadski asks. Piña Colada occurs to the barman. Juice of a ripe pineapple, ice, sugar, coconut cream, lime juice and Bacardi rum.

"Something for women and children," Levadski says, "and for real men."

"We will take it," Mr. Witzturn says, "Piña Colada cheers everyone up and paradoxically has a depressing effect on cheerful dispositions. In the sixties, Piña Colada was the magic potion for young widows." Mr. Witzturn's nose, like a wooden arrow in the wind, turns in the direction of the Russian. "They had barely overcome their grief, barely felt the stirrings of a *joie de vivre*, when after having overindulged in drink, out of the blue, they jumped off railway bridges. Some ran right out of their local bar, single-minded, straight to the river, without having paid their bills."

"I understand little of women," Levadski whispers to Mr. Witzturn, who promptly turns towards the white-skinned foreigner again.

"The cocktails are not that important for the novel." The Russian's words sound muted, as if she were holding a folded handkerchief in front of her mouth. "More important are, perhaps, the conversations at the bar that my hero thinks he is engaging in. The probability is very high, I fear, that there is nobody for this ripe old man to have a conversation with. I personally would like my hero not to be on his own. But it would be too simple," she sighs into the bartender's back, who is stretching to reach a bottle of Balvenie. "Too simple and too sad."

"Too sad if he had a drinking companion?" The bartender turns to face her; the bottle of Balvenie turns out to be a half empty bottle of port.

"Everyone dies in their own way," the Russian smiles, licking the sugared rim of her cocktail glass. A crack, long and thin like a luminous root, snakes up the length of the glass, into which the mouth and the Russian's shock of hair have already disappeared. The rest of her body appears to disintegrate into specks of dust in the darkness and never to have existed.

With a creaking sound, Levadski turns his head towards Mr. Witzturn, who is in the middle of discreetly adjusting his nose. "What I don't understand is why we have to dress warmly for the Neo-Neoromantic age." Mr. Witzturn grins.

"Because it will exercise a painful but also a salutary blow to reigning reason. The occidental civilization, you will agree with me, is ruthlessly being roasted in the sun of naked facts. The tree of belief has withered away in our materialist world — it no longer offers shade. To survive, man will remember Romanticism and have to seek it in other spheres. He will seek it beneath the roots of trees and in groundwater. He will seek and find, and in this way return to nature. That is what my reason tells me, Mr. Levadski."

"Oh, reason," Levadski juts out his lower lip. "I often think to myself that if genuine terror exists, then it is the terror of reason. It is reason that doesn't allow the most beautiful fruits of the imagination to mature ..."

"My sentiments entirely," says Mr. Witzturn, "my sentiments entirely, dear friend, to hell with reason." He wants to add something, scratches his head and then changes his mind. "We have light!" The bartender's voice sounds more cheerful than it is.

What a shame, thinks Levadski, just when I really feel like I am thinking more clearly.

"We have light," the bartender says triumphantly. With a wet thumb and forefinger he approaches the round brackets holding the candles and puts out one after the other. In the mirror, Levadski sees that the white dinner jacket belongs to a man no longer youthful in appearance, but with attentive and infinitely weary eyes. We have light, the bartender seems to whisper to himself. Light ...

5
Zimmer / Room 501–521

"Pharaoh eagle-owl, parasitic jaeger, orange-banded snapper tyrant, Costa's Hummingbird … Well, these aren't special birds, it's only their names that make them special, lend them a certain tone, dignity and maybe gravitas. But what's in a name? Everything, and already blown away by the wind, scattered to the wind like sand."

"You are sad because your friend has left?"

"Happy and at the same time sad. I met a special person, Habib, a person like every other and yet special to me, because I met him, consciously met him. That I did it consciously was of course not obvious to me. It is only now that I am conscious of it. I don't know whether you understand me."

Habib gives his round head a good scratch. "Yes, we often forget that every person we meet could become a special person. For us."

"And through us, or is that asking too much?"

"Yes, maybe that too," Habib nods. "It was only when I was looking after my paralyzed father, as fate would have it, that I really met him, even though for years he raised me, saw me naked, disciplined me. Our real encounter happened when he lay helpless before me and I learned to hold back my tears while feeding him and changing him. It often felt like he knew about this battle within me and he too held back his tears, other tears, tears of pride and joy that would have been completely out of place."

"Why?"

"Because he should have been embarrassed or grit his teeth in anger. After all, I was his son, doing women's work. But he was proud nevertheless, I am sure of that."

"Perhaps your father became a real father through his pride and his joy, a better person."

"A son who does women's work!" Habib laughs. "Evidently he had to suffer a stroke in order to grasp that it wasn't something dishonorable."

"You see, I feel like that today, I am sad and yet I feel happy. I will never see this gentleman again. And perhaps I will forget him soon. But it won't mean anything, the genuine remains nameless, incoherent and as reliable as a Swiss watchmaker's clock."

"It's still early, I bet your friend is at the breakfast table and doesn't dare hide behind the morning paper out of fear that he will miss you."

"In his place I wouldn't come to breakfast. Why cloud the memory of yesterday with so much daylight. Everything that wanted to be said was said. Or so I assume, even though there's much I can't remember anymore."

"I am happy to go and see whether your friend is at the breakfast table. Or can I pass on a letter from you to him. A card."

"You are kind, Habib."

Black spider webs burgeon in Habib's nostrils, a tiny insect intermittently twitches in one of them. If he were to sneeze, the little thing would fly out of his nose and trace a high arc, Levadski thinks. He wants to say something nice to the butler but he remains silently slumped in his armchair. Habib, hands folded, appears to be waiting for something.

"I am an old man," Levadski interrupts the silence. His voice sounds muted, as if the walls of the room were thickly carpeted and not fitted with silk wallpaper. "I am an old man," he repeats firmly, "I will die soon." A laughing matter too, thinks Levadski. "I will die," he says once more. Habib's chin sinks to his chest, as if he wants to sleep.

"I am not in this hotel for fun," Levadski continues, "I don't want you to form the wrong impression of me." Habib's eyes are two fresh graves covered in hoarfrost.

"I came back to the city of my childhood. Not even childhood. I returned to the city of my blessed mother. In order to die, so I thought. But I don't think the money will suffice for that. My God, have I grown so tough, too tough for death?" Habib looks like he is fast asleep. A fly is circling on an invisible turntable above him.

"Even the fact that I deceived my old apartment and became a traitor, an adulterer, is no longer painful. That is how tough I have become. I swapped it for a luxurious lover, for this suite, for grandeur and the strangely delightful view – over there the pharmacy, a kiosk, a taxi stand, the streetcar tracks, hooded crows' nests. With the stroke of a pen I eliminated all those shared years with my apartment. But it is not painful anymore, there is something else that is painful. The joy." Habib nods, his head rolls to one side, his tongue, a little red flag, is peeking out of his mouth.

"I did everything, everything wrong, you can't just suddenly die like I was intending to. I am not in pain. Yet, what should I do, what should I do Habib, I have to die, I have to give up the ghost somehow." A young, almost transparent eel snakes out of Habib's mouth. The butler sighs deeply in his sleep.

"I wish I could call my family doctor now and tell

him, It is all wrong, I don't have any complaints, I can't for the life of me die, Professor Doctor, but his number is in my notebook, which is lying beside my telephone. It is an old fashioned model, I don't know whether you would even know the type. The telephone is gathering dust in my apartment, which I swapped for this suite here. For death in luxury. Where Death is, I would like to know. In the city by the sea, on a park bench, where I was in the habit of sitting for hours on end until I grew cold. Maybe Death is sitting there and spitting on its scythe. Is sitting and spitting its hissing saliva ... Even if I call my family doctor and report on my completely inappropriate condition, what use is it to me? I wouldn't feel any worse. Of course I could accuse him of having made me the false promise of death, but what would I gain? That I decided to celebrate my infirmity and my approaching end in luxury is my problem. That I can't just insist on languishing and dying is also my problem. What fault is it of the doctor's that I can't go back? That I can't stay here either? The money will suffice for a few more weeks. And then?" In Habib's deep silence the wind is playing with the well bucket. A mouse is gnawing at the rope.

"My apartment is locked. Dust clings to the books of my library, and the little radio, and to Radio World Harmony. Dust and ash from the bridges that are burning. My good old apartment. There is no going back anymore, Habib. I feel fine, the end is not in sight. Do you understand what that means?" In Habib's silence, cannons are being stuffed with gunpowder, a crow flies over a sun-drenched plain, a messenger between two enemy camps. It is fall.

"Not so long ago I stepped into the golden elevator of the hotel. It was a delight to hover in the elevator. I felt like I was in my mother's lap, beyond good and evil. A possibility occurred to me then. I imagined dying a

Who Is Martha?

more pleasant death than the one prescribed me by my illness. A beautiful, horrific death, unworthy of a scientist. A magical disappearance. I imagined riding up to the last floor and looking out the window into an empty crow's nest. In that instant I am dead." Habib's eyelids twitch in his sleep. He is running for his life.

"I never looked in empty bird's nests, Habib. From the moment I started admiring birds I always knew: I can do what I like, I can observe birds through a telescope, I can sketch them, count them, play to them on a whistle, I can roast them and eat them, make handles for my desk drawers from their bare bones – I could do everything. But if one day I should look through the bare twigs of trees into an empty nest, I would be done for." A sleepy smile blossoms on Habib's face. Levadski places his hand on his heart.

"A forbidden fruit that means more than death. The look into an empty bird's nest obliterates everything: my curiosity for life would have been erased, my *joie de vivre*, my respect for a miracle of creation – the bird. Looking into a friend's chamber pot is nothing by comparison. Then I looked around in the elevator and scrutinized my four mirror-images, they all panted down my neck and said: Let it be, my friend, go and enjoy breakfast instead, until you can no longer get up. Wander from window to window in your suite, watch the bustle in the street, the old ladies with their comical lapdogs, after all it makes you happy, doesn't it? I glanced up at the mirrored ceiling of the elevator. Ride up to the fifth floor, my fifth double whispered to me, look into a bird's nest, give yourself the last blow, rob yourself of joy, die!" Habib's mouth twitches, as if he has bitten into an electric cable.

"I suspect that my dear departed father looked into an empty bird's nest before taking his life in the forest. Out of boredom. He was a dreamer, but who knows who he really was? Perhaps, and that would be far worse, he planned and carried it out consciously because he foresaw the future, the war, the revolution, hunger. The most pleasant conception is that there was no bullet, just a look – a blue titmouse whirs past my father's breaking eye, to a distant and unreachable branch ... While I was hovering in the elevator on the way to breakfast, I understood my father, whom I never knew. For a split second I felt a deep sense of understanding within me. That's how it is, Habib." Levadski wipes his mouth and carries on talking.

"What I am left with, in my situation, is hope in the power of thought. There is, after all, an internal alarm clock. I often used to get up by telling myself before going to sleep, Tomorrow at seven on the dot. And at seven o'clock on the dot I would leap out of bed as if I had been stung by bees. Do you know that internal alarm clock?" In Habib's silence, flags flutter, spurs jangle, clumps of grass are whirled about by horse hooves, slowly, like corals overgrown with seaweed.

"All I can do is wind that internal clock up again and rely on it: drop dead in two weeks. What do you say to that?" Black smoke pours from Habib's mouth, a barn full of pigs and piglets is burning. It is wartime. Wartime or just a storm.

"There is nothing else I can do but trust in this clock, trust in the power of thought ..." A question that loses its urgency is written in Habib's wide-open eyes. They are hazy, dream-veiled images which remain an unfathomable secret to himself. A glance at the watch above the white glove – a day has passed, or maybe even two, and still Habib remains seated. Day after day he enters Levadski's suite and stays sitting on a pouf with no back support, the most beautiful piece of furniture in Levadski's suite.

Levadski pulls his handkerchief that looks like a trampled concertina from his pocket and dries his forehead.

Who Is Martha?

"There is something I can't get out of my head. Habib. It was a long time ago. I was on the way home with my mother. Sometimes we came across a farmer who let us sit up on his team of elk. The further we got, the more astonished the farmers were who gave us a ride. The elk turned into bony farm horses. Summer turned to winter. We rode on the roof of an icy train, too, but most of the time we went on foot. We walked along the snowy rails, wrapped in the furs of farm animals we had raised in a kolkhoz, fed and then skinned. We knew we had a long journey ahead of us, straight across Eurasia, you understand what that means? I was your age. Although half your size. We didn't eat much in exile, but healthily. Mainly mare's milk and cheese. I assume that's why I lost my teeth when I was very old and not at the age of fifty like my colleagues.

Levadski licks the roof of his mouth with his tongue, as if he were counting the ribs. "On one occasion, when we were following the rails, I heard a noise. The leader of a flock of swans was counting its team by pronouncing every member's name in a wild trumpet call. Just as I turned my head towards the sky one of the swans flew into a power line. I saw it fall like a shooting star, only much more rapidly. My mother let out a cry, the swans flew on in a tapered formation in the direction of the arctic to breed, as if nothing had happened. After searching for a long time we found the swan in a boggy field. A bloody bone protruded from its feathers. It looked like a pale bellboy with a crude wooden sword. We came closer. The swan, its face distorted in fear and pain, dragged itself further and further away from us. We had no intention of catching it. It was impossible to fix it, but something forced us to follow the animal, with respect, slowly, so that it had a chance to escape. Why did we torment the bird like that? Because we were mesmerized. It was, if I may put it this way, one of the most peaceful moments in my life. How should I explain it?"

"Your story reminds me of my father's last days," Habib says, clearing his throat. "I noticed he was preparing to die. It was a similar magic, a similar peace. His apathy acquired new dimensions from one day to the next. While he lay there rigidly before me and I read aloud to him, I had the feeling that my words were not falling into an empty well, as usual, but were colliding with a wall of carpet. I realized, my father was no longer listening. He no longer needed to. He no longer needed my living voice or the living word. I would have liked to feel insulted or at least sad, but something larger would not allow for this petty feeling. Now I know: it was the magic of farewell, a promise that wanted to fulfill itself far from this world. And that this promise would be of no use to me in the here and now, that was an elevating feeling. More elevating than what we call love."

"I presume it is the same thing." Clouds of tenderness drift across Levadski's moist eyes. He sees the swan, its yellow-black beak slightly parted, a wooden sword clamped beneath its arm. The bat of an eyelash, and the swan is already dragging itself across the field. "Only love can be that elevating. I am completely sure of it. Love for its own sake. Perhaps you are right, Habib, What's in a name? Yes, what's in a name: In the end we always mean one and the same thing. We mean well, don't we?"

Habib nods and gently clearing his throat, adjusts the cap already sitting perfectly on his head. "My name, for example, means Dear One, but I don't think of that when I hear my name. Habib here, Habib there. I know people mean well. Even if I my name were Stick or Idiot, it wouldn't bother me."

"You are a good person, my dear Habib. Do you mind if I call you that?"

"No, why?"

Who Is Martha?

"Because it's a tautology, like sweet sugar." Once more Habib's fingertips touch the cap on his head. The further the swan drags itself through the mud, the bigger its crushed body grows, until it gets up and stands perfectly straight – a pale bellboy with oriental eyes.

"It would be different if you called me Habiba by mistake. For your sake, I would have to make you aware that Habiba is the feminine form of Habib. But that wouldn't bother me either, because I would know you mean me."

"For my sake?"

"Yes, because you seem to be an inquisitive person."

"Do you know why it is that swallows prefer to make their nests on the roof beams of horse stables?"

"Because they like the smell of the stables?"

"The bird's sense of smell is only slightly developed."

"Then why?"

"Perhaps it is because the horses have a calming effect on these restless birds, and there is always something to eat in a stable, loads of insects. I have always been interested in such relationships. Inquisitive or not. I have observed the finely woven fabric of the universe, thread by thread. From the insect to the swallow I found certainty that I too must belong to it." Levadski remains still and listens to his own thoughts. "Irrespective of how lonely you might feel from time to time, irrespective." Two floes of ice project from Habib's rosy mouth. With arms crossed he is rocking back and forth on his seat.

"A beautiful song is priceless. At home people like to sing, and for no particular reason. Here they point a finger at you if you think of singing in public."

"We should let the birds set an example! A clever soliloquy, like the birds demonstrate in song, can't possibly harm us humans either. On the contrary. You know, Habib, if there is something I regret from the bottom of my heart, it's that I do not sing."

"Why don't you sing?"

"It's not that I am not enthusiastic about song. I have just always had a despondency in me that forbids me to do it. It's clear I have always sung to myself, inside me. But it is something different when you think your own soul out loud, with the volume turned up. Birds do it, Habib, it is their way of conducting a monologue."

"Do they?"

"You can bet your life. Birds innocently give their souls up to the wind and to the entire world when they sing. Their thought is anchored in the structure of the world."

"What about our thought?"

"Not long ago I was on the verge of believing that human beings keep their thoughts secret from the world. Humans lie, even if they are being honest. They lie because they have fallen out of the framework of the world, from the tree of life ... Only a few days ago I was convinced that human beings were worse than animals because of it. After the few chance acquaintances made under this roof – What is chance anyway, Habib? – it dawned on me that I was mistaken. We are not worse nor fundamentally very different from birds. A part of the same animate world."

Levadski carefully exhales. "I am not talking about externalities, Habib. At no point in evolution have we ever been able to keep up with the birds, with their hollow bones and featherweight. Just think, the Quetzalcoatlus, one of the largest flying reptiles in the Cretaceous period, had a wingspan of fifty feet and weighed as much as you do. What an astonishing experiment of nature. In comparison, the crown of creation is a laughingstock." Habib laughs.

"Do you mean us?"

The picture of the swan lands in Levadski's eye like a grain of dust. He rubs it in slow circular motions. The swan stands upright with its wooden sword beak and the tiny bellboy on its arm. Holy Mary!

"Think about it, Habib, how many millions of years later did we arrive at the air-filled tire, when all that would have been necessary was to observe the birds more closely, to dissect them and not just eat them. We should not have stuck the feathers on our heads as jewelry, but have examined them carefully. Or the behavior of birds, how they eat and hunt, live and breathe. A little more relaxed and patient, and I bet we would not have fallen from the tree of life so calamitously."

"We compensated for the fall with fantastic inventions like the telephone, refridgerator and automobile," Habib says triumphantly. Levadski makes a dismissive gesture.

"A product that arises out of desperation and wounded pride cannot be good. The hummingbird, the size of a bumblebee, never invented anything in its life, but in a long process has perfected itself beyond the limits of our imagination. Fifty wing beats per second! We can only wiggle our ears. But I am not talking about externalities. What is at stake is the art, the art of existence." With a silver rippling gaze, Habib appears to be seeping into the essence of things he does not understand.

"I must have been dazzled, believing all this time that we were different from birds. We may have invented the fridge and the telephone – perhaps that was a necessary deviation. But in doing so we took a long way around the tree of life from which we fell and to which we will hopefully return. Perhaps it really did have to happen this way." Levadski's voice is shaking.

"Good things come to those who wait," Habib says, shrugging his shoulders.

"Now here we stand again, in front of the magic tree, the last representatives of the evolutionary line of hominids. We are so lonely, Habib."

"You are not lonely."

"We are so lonely, so terribly lonely. Like the horses, who are the last representatives of equids. Not surprising that we have fraternized with the horse. We are the last."

Gigantic floes of ice collide with each other in Habib's eyes. Crystals of ice flash like daggers. With a sigh Habib lets his head drop to his shoulder.

"Think about it, Habib, think about it, there have always been several species of humans. Neanderthals and Cro-Magnons and many others, God knows how many there really were. Now we are alone. And have been for almost 35,000 years."

"Not alone, no ..." groans Habib.

Levadski peers into Habib's round face. The cawing swan with the wooden dagger beak and the bellboy on his arm drags itself to the edge of the ice floe.

"We are the only survivors of our line of ancestors, Habib, a temporary appearance on earth." Habib listlessly rubs his cheek against the padded shoulder of his butler jacket. The wind plays in the à-la-Liszt hairstyle of the swan. Motionless, the animal stands on the edge of the ice floe, silently snapping its wooden beak open and shut, as if in prayer. The wing on which the bellboy sleeps is a bloody bone.

"Not alone ..." Levadski hears Habib hoarsely telling the wind in defiance. "What's in a name? You yourself said, a name is nothing. We do not bear a name, it bears us." Habib's voice is lost in the squawking of the seagulls.

"Oh, Habib, you are a precious young man, you are right. Whether hominids or equids, they are only names, aren't they." Levadski nods and shakes off a little ice floe that is obscuring his vision. Another and another. "When I think of centaurs and sphinxes, of mythology where men and animals were one ... all of it has a genuine core. The definition of animal is essentially a foolish idea. That it is a lower being, a thing, a non-person. High time we

Who Is Martha?

abandoned this anthropocentric way of thinking that is thousands of years old. Heaven is meant to be sublime? Don't make me laugh." Levadski laughs and chokes.

"Paradise," the butler's voice is a brown trout, "has always been alive with animals," a brown trout in the belly of a snake, "go to the museum if you don't believe me."

The snake, like a rapid little stream, curls around Levadski's forest hut, nuzzles up to Levadski's mother's feet, to the red shoes with their buckles which, blinded by the water, Levadski can't tell if they're rusty or golden.

"In the museum you can see for yourself that earthly paradise has always been represented in the same way by painters of all ages and peoples: it is alive with animals."

Smiling, Levadski tilts his head to one side. "I won't go to the museum any more, Habib. I believe you."

Chemotherapy and radiation to prolong life (several months) recommended. Severe weight loss, night sweats, fever, metastasis, feelings of faintness. In the advanced stages: metastases in the brain, liver, skeleton; skeletal pain, morphine, tablets or patch, Fentanyl, Methadone.

What am I to do with that?

You have the choice.

I have nothing.

I am fine. No complaints, nothing. I can hardly feel anything. I am a feather, I could say. Now I know what it is to molt, Professor Doctor. Experienced it myself, Professor Doctor. Levadski gropes his way to the window. That darkness has descended, he didn't notice. Has he been sleeping? It is evening. An evening in fall, with hooded crows. Like in a coffeehouse, Levadski smiles, that's the way they are sitting there on the branches, back to back, the hooded crows, like at tables in a coffeehouse, airing their behinds, as if they intended to pull their wallets from their plumage and pay ... An evening in fall with hooded crows and a bird's nest. Levadski picks up his opera glasses and tries to look into the crow's nest. But his window is too low, and the nest is too high.

Drop dead in two weeks ... Habib did not say a word to that. He has always had something to say to everything, and now? Each to his own, my mother would have said. She would have removed her glasses, blinked at me through her shrunken eyes and laughed. Without glasses her eyes were naked; naked and dull. God knows whether they were green, gray or blue. But they were naked without glasses. As naked as I must be for others without my dentures. Where are they all? Where is Habib? Shall I ring for him?

Levadski's gaze wanders to the telephone and the button with the butler. On his unwavering calm hand he is balancing a tray with steaming coffee cups. Over the last few days Levadski has not pressed the button, but Habib

210   *Who Is Martha?*

has come anyway, appeared in the doorframe every day, swearing to the beauty of the morning. And now? Levadski pokes his head through the curtains. An illuminated streetcar with two passengers drives past: a lady with a puffball hair-do is wiping a child's nose. A rocking horse hangs over it like a threatening cloud. A balloon on a thin thread, which Levadski can only divine from his lookout post.

Levadski makes his way to the door. The northern bald ibis flies over the Alps, headed south. Its foster father in a small plane leading the way. Inaudible is the sound of the inner clock ticking, inaudible the turning of the propellers. He steps out. The babble of voices spreads out from the foyer over the gallery, like a scent. In two steps Levadski reaches the elevator and presses the button, keeps on pressing until the elevator arrives. The bartender with his mixing glass in hand steps aside smiling.

"Good day, did you sleep well?" Levadski thanks him, he had a nice dream. "Which floor?"

"Five." The bartender smiles and lets his forefinger glide across all the buttons. A rascal, Levadski thinks.

On the first floor the bartender gets out and turns left, shaking his glass vigorously. The chambermaid from Novi Pazar nimbly walks past the open elevator door and waves to Levadski by raising and lowering her wicker basket. It is exactly the same movement that Levadski once saw in the window of a lighthouse in a spa town on the Black Sea, shortly before a black-headed gull ripped a piece of cake from his hand. You stole my joy! he most likely shouted at it, stamping his foot, red in the face. The elevator door closes with a slight squeak, the chambermaid is singing in the corridor. Levadski can barely understand her, but he can hear her, he can make out the words: Joy. Beautiful spark of divinity? He dives towards the elevator door and presses his ear against the cool metal. He must have misheard.

On the second floor the elevator jolts to a halt. The door opens hesitantly. If only the bartender had not pressed all the buttons, Levadski thinks. The rascal ... Once more the barman is standing before him. Levadski steps aside. "Sleep well?" The bartender thanks him by giving his mixing glass a short, energetic shake.

"I dreamed about you," he says, "that you honored me with a visit to the bar."

"Really?"

"Yes, and then a hatch opened behind my bar that looked exactly like this elevator, and you suddenly wanted to go to your room and I accompanied you downstairs. Have you already pressed?"

"You already pressed them – all the buttons."

"Nonsense, I only dusted the buttons, but now!" The bartender's forefinger reaches towards the flat golden buttons. He hastily presses 3 and 4, applies a certain thoroughness to 5.

The bartender gets out on the third floor. "Good luck," he says to Levadski, rattling his mixing glass. And again the chambermaid walks past the open elevator door. Levadski looks in her basket. What is lying inside, covered by a white napkin, reminds him of raspberries. And again the oscillating motion of her hand. The chambermaid, so it seems to Levadski, turns the corner singing. The door of the elevator closes. There is no mistake, she is singing, she really is singing! Again Levadski presses his ear to the door. Along with the squeaking of the cable and the wheels he can clearly hear the chambermaid singing.

Drunk with fiery rapture
All men become ...
Where your gentle wing rests

"Brothers! Brothers, it goes!" Levadski shouts, clasping his forehead. That's the Ninth. She is singing Beethoven's Ninth!

All beings drink joy
Both the good and the evil

"Draw joy from nature's breast," Levadski softly joins in.

"Be embraced, millions," the chambermaid replies.

"Take this kiss for all the world," Levadski sings embarrassed through the door crack.

On the fourth floor there is not a soul to be seen. Levadski pokes his head out of the elevator. Only the crystal drops of the wall lights are tinkling softly. Powerful singing.

Joyously, as his suns speed
Hasten brothers on your way

It must be coming from the *Musikverein*, thinks Levadski, the singing, I can't think of any other explanation. Unless there is an entire choir hiding in the hotel ... A red feather twirls through the air, while the door of the elevator slowly closes. Or am I mistaken? Perhaps the house is on fire? A blood-bespattered bird feather and a spark of fire are not the same thing. But it is of no importance now whether it is burning.

It has been snowing on the fifth floor. Levadski gets out, his steps crunching across a carpet of feathers. It was most likely the barman who wanted to surprise me, Levadski is amazed. Who else would have emptied so many pillows onto the floor? Only that rascal of a bartender, wanting to give me a special treat up here on the fifth floor. As if it were my birthday! While Levadski makes a pathway for himself through the white splendor, he feels a slight apprehension. Is it really fall? If it really were my birthday today, it would have to be spring. Or, fall? Levadski remains rooted to the spot. A piece of down is stuck to his lower lip. Another piece of down covers his left eye. He wipes his jacket sleeve across his face. The feathers in the corridor have suddenly disappeared, blown away by the wind. Whether summer or winter, the reality is that the fifth floor doesn't have any windows! How am I to look into the empty nest if there are no windows? His hand pressed to his chest, Levadski walks along the corridor. His dentures are missing. Missing, like the drinking stick he has forgotten in his room. As if he knew he could do without the services of those accessories today. Why take fright then? Not a single window, who would have thought it?

Joyously as his suns speed
Through Heaven's glorious order
Exulting as a knight in victory

The voice of the chambermaid sounds behind one of the numerous doors. Levadski balls his hand into a fist. But he will not knock. It is joy that spreads through him like a cramp. A muscle ache such as he has never before experienced. Levadski drags himself from door to door with fists clenched in pleasure. Behind every door the chambermaid is singing. Behind every door Levadski hears her song.

Be embraced millions
Brothers above the canopy of stars
He must dwell beyond the stars

Breathing heavily, Levadski comes to a halt at the end

of the corridor. There is nowhere to go from here. Or is there? A fire door stands ajar. A small stairway leads upward. The chambermaid's singing, which seems to be coming from everywhere, blinds him, whips his eyes, his face. He wants to kneel, to fall and disappear into the ground, but he is holding onto the door handle and looking up at the top of the stairs, where in the half-darkness he can make out the oily leaves of a rubber plant and a door, which, as he observes it, slowly begins to open.

Mr. Levadski?
Yes.
Mr. Levadski, what is your first name?
Luka. Luka Stepanovich.
When were you …
Yes.
When were you born?
I don't know.
What year?
The year that Martha died.
Who is Martha?
Her name was Martha!
Levadski is staring intently. The door slowly opens. The leaves of the rubber plant give a swaying nod.
Her name was Martha.
Who is Martha, Mr. Levadski?
The door opens wider and wider. A beam of light falls onto the floor like a panel of blond linden wood.
I don't know.
Was Martha your mother's name?
I don't know.
When did Martha die?
When I was born.
When was that?
I don't know.

Mr. Levadski?

Her name was Martha. Levadski screws up his eyes. He wants to see further, deeper, behind the light bursting through the open door. And further still. Further than possible. Further than conceivable.

Mr. Levadski?

Her name was Martha, Martha! Levadski bows in front of the pane of glass separating him from the girl, and throws up. Her name was Martha, Martha. And throws up. Martha, her name was Martha. Levadski throws up in front of Martha, a second before the man with the moustache kisses her hand, in front of the chocolate cake, the cake that remains untouched, in front of the girl's eyes, eyes that penetrate everything, the window pane, Levadski, hunched over, who can't stop vomiting, can't stop turning his insides out.

Mr. Levadski?

Yes.

You were born on?

Yes.

You were born?

Mr. Levadski?

Mr. ...

I owe my inspiration and ideas to:

Malcolm Tait, Olive Tayler: *Vögel, Geflügelte Wunder, fantastische Schwärmereien und ordentlichen Ornithologie.* Translated from the English and edited by Arnulf Conradi. With a foreword by Hark Bohm. Hamburg: Hoffmann und Campe 2008; Pascal Picq: *Die schönste Geschichte der Tiere. Von den Geheimnissen des Lebens.* Translated from the French by Friedel Schröder and Marita Kluxen-Schröder. Berglisch Gladbach: Lübbe 2001; Peter Hayman, Philip Burton: *Das goldene Kosmos-Vogelbuch. Europas Vögel – bestimmen verstehen schützen.* Kosmos Gesellschaft für Naturfreunde 1988; *Das Reader's Digest Buch der Vogelwelt Mitteleuropas.* Stuttgart: Verlag Das Beste 1973; Bernhard Grzimek (Editor)*: Grzimeks Tierleben.* Enzyklopädie des Tierreichs. Volumes. 7, 8, 9. Zurich: Kindler 1968ff.; E. Thomas Gilliard, Georg Steinbacher: *Vögel.* Knaurs Tierreich in Farben. München, Zurich: Droemersche Verlagsanstalt 1959; Karl von Frisch; *Verständliche Wissenschaft.* Volume 1: *Aus dem Leben der Bienen.* Berlin: Verlag Julius Springer 1927; Karl Krall: *Denkende Tiere. Beiträge zur Tierseelenkunde auf Grund eigener Versuche.* Leipzig: Verlag Friedrich Engelmann 1912; Claus Obalski (Editor): *Taktlosigkeiten, Komponisten als Kritiker.* Munich: Obalski & Astor 1986; Alfred Brendel: *Nachdenken über Musik.* With an interview by Jeremy Siepmann. Munich: Piper 1977 *Das große Buch der Musik.* Freiburg i.B.: Herder 1962.

I Called Him Necktie by Milena Michiko Flašar

Twenty-year-old Taguchi Hiro has spent the last two years of his life living as a hikikomori—a shut-in who never leaves his room and has no human interaction—in his parents' home in Tokyo. As Hiro tentatively decides to reenter the world, he spends his days observing life from a park bench. Gradually he makes friends with Ohara Tetsu, a salaryman who has lost his job. The two discover in their sadness a common bond. This beautiful novel is moving, unforgettable, and full of surprises.

Guys Like Me by Dominique Fabre

Dominique Fabre, born in Paris and a lifelong resident of the city, exposes the shadowy, anonymous lives of many who inhabit the French capital. In this quiet, subdued tale, a middle-aged office worker, divorced and alienated from his only son, meets up with two childhood friends who are similarly adrift. He's looking for a second act to his mournful life, seeking the harbor of love and a true connection with his son. Set in palpably real Paris streets that feel miles away from the City of Light, a stirring novel of regret and absence, yet not without a glimmer of hope.

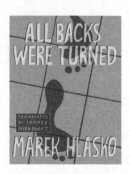

All Backs Were Turned by Marek Hlasko

Two desperate friends – on the edge of the law – travel to the southern Israeli city of Eilat to find work. There, Dov Ben Dov, the handsome native Israeli with a reputation for causing trouble, and Israel, his sidekick, stay with Ben Dov's younger brother, Little Dov, who has enough trouble of his own. Local toughs are encroaching on Little Dov's business, and he enlists his older brother to drive them away. It doesn't help that a beautiful German widow is rooming next door. A story of passion, deception, violence, and betrayal, conveyed in hard-boiled prose reminiscent of Hammett and Chandler.

COCAINE BY PITIGRILLI

Paris in the 1920s – dizzy and decadent. Where a young man can make a fortune with his wits ... unless he is led into temptation. Cocaine's dandified hero Tito Arnaudi invents lurid scandals and gruesome deaths, and sells these stories to the newspapers. But his own life becomes even more outrageous when he acquires three demanding mistresses. Elegant, witty and wicked, Pitigrilli's classic novel was first published in Italian in 1921 and retains its venom even today.

THE GOOD LIFE ELSEWHERE BY VLADIMIR LORCHENKOV

The very funny - and very sad - story of a group of villagers and their tragicomic efforts to emigrate from Europe's most impoverished nation to Italy for work. An Orthodox priest is deserted by his wife for an art-dealing atheist; a mechanic redesigns his tractor for travel by air and sea; and thousands of villagers take to the road on a modern-day religious crusade to make it to the Italian Promised Land. A country where 25 percent of its population works abroad, remittances make up nearly 40 percent of GDP, and alcohol consumption per capita is the world's highest – Moldova surely has its problems. But, as Lorchenkov vividly shows, it's also a country whose residents don't give up easily.

FANNY VON ARNSTEIN: DAUGHTER OF THE ENLIGHTENMENT BY HILDE SPIEL

In 1776 Fanny von Arnstein, the daughter of the Jewish master of the royal mint in Berlin, came to Vienna as an 18-year-old bride. She married a financier to the Austro-Hungarian imperial court, and hosted an ever more splendid salon which attracted luminaries of the day. Spiel's elegantly written and carefully researched biography provides a vivid portrait of a passionate woman who advocated for the rights of Jews, and illuminates a central era in European cultural and social history.

KILLING THE SECOND DOG BY MAREK HLASKO

Two down-and-out Polish con men living in Israel in the 1950s scam an American widow visiting the country. Robert, who masterminds the scheme, and Jacob, who acts it out, are tough, desperate men, exiled from their native land and adrift in the hot, nasty underworld of Tel Aviv. Robert arranges for Jacob to run into the widow who has enough trouble with her young son to keep her occupied all day. What follows is a story of romance, deception, cruelty and shame. Hlasko's writing combines brutal realism with smoky, hardboiled dialogue, in a bleak world where violence is the norm and love is often only an act.

THE MISSING YEAR OF JUAN SALVATIERRA BY PEDRO MAIRAL

At the age of nine, Juan Salvatierra became mute following a horse riding accident. At twenty, he began secretly painting a series of canvases on which he detailed six decades of life in his village on Argentina's frontier with Uruguay. After his death, his sons return to deal with their inheritance: a shed packed with rolls over two miles long. But an essential roll is missing. A search ensues that illuminates links between art and life, with past family secrets casting their shadows on the present.

SOME DAY BY SHEMI ZARHIN

On the shores of Israel's Sea of Galilee lies the city of Tiberias, a place bursting with sexuality and longing for love. The air is saturated with smells of cooking and passion. Some Day is a gripping family saga, a sensual and emotional feast that plays out over decades. This is an enchanting tale about tragic fates that disrupt families and break our hearts. Zarhin's hypnotic writing renders a painfully delicious vision of individual lives behind Israel's larger national story.

New Vessel Press

To purchase these titles and for more information please visit
newvesselpress.com.